"You do know what [   ] all work and no play, don't you?"

He regarded her seriously. "That it gets the job done?"

She groaned. "No, that it makes for a very dull guy."

A dangerous glint appeared in his eyes. "You think I'm boring?"

"Not boring, just limited. Under other circumstances, I might be tempted to try and change that."

"Oh? How?"

"Maybe one of these days I'll give you a list of my recommendations," she said. "Will you pay any attention to them?"

"I might," he said solemnly. "What would my reward be?"

"More fun," she said at once.

He grinned. "You'll have to provide more incentive than that."

"Such as?"

"Will I get the girl?"

Gina shuddered at the penetrating look in his eyes. "I suppose that depends."

"On?"

"On how badly you want her."

"I'm beginning to wonder about that myself."

2601

Dear Reader,

International bestselling author Diana Palmer needs no introduction. Widely known for her sensual and emotional storytelling, and with more than forty million copies of her books in print, she is one of the genre's most treasured authors. And this month, Special Edition is proud to bring you the exciting conclusion to her SOLDIERS OF FORTUNE series. *The Last Mercenary* is the thrilling tale of a mercenary hero risking it all for love. Between the covers is the passion and adventure you've come to expect from Diana Palmer!

Speaking of passion and adventure, don't miss *To Catch a Thief* by Sherryl Woods in which trouble—in the form of attorney Rafe O'Donnell—follows Gina Petrillo home for her high school reunion and sparks fly.... Things are hotter than the Hatfields and McCoys in Laurie Paige's *When I Dream of You*— when heat turns to passion between two families that have been feuding for three generations!

Is a heroine's love strong enough to heal a hero scarred inside and out? Find out in *Another Man's Children* by Christine Flynn. And when an interior designer pretends to be a millionaire's lover, will *Her Secret Affair* lead to a public proposal? Don't miss *An Abundance of Babies* by Marie Ferrarella—in which double the babies and double the love could be just what an estranged couple needs to bring them back together.

This is the last month to enter our Silhouette Makes You a Star contest, so be sure to look inside for details. And as always, enjoy these fantastic stories celebrating life, love and family.

Best,
Karen Taylor Richman
Senior Editor

Please address questions and book requests to:
Silhouette Reader Service
U.S.: 3010 Walden Ave., P.O. Box 1325, Buffalo, NY 14269
Canadian: P.O. Box 609, Fort Erie, Ont. L2A 5X3

Sherryl Woods

TO CATCH A THIEF

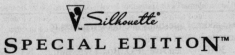

Silhouette®

SPECIAL EDITION™

Published by Silhouette Books

America's Publisher of Contemporary Romance

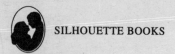 SILHOUETTE BOOKS

ISBN 0-373-24418-5

TO CATCH A THIEF

Copyright © 2001 by Sherryl Woods

Visit Silhouette at www.eHarlequin.com

Printed in U.S.A.

SHERRYL WOODS

has written more than seventy-five romances and mysteries in the past twenty years. She also operates her own bookstore, Potomac Sunrise, in Colonial Beach, Virginia, where readers from around the country stop by to discuss her favorite topic—books. If you can't visit Sherryl at her store, then be sure to drop her a note at P.O. Box 490326, Key Biscayne, FL 33149 or check out her website at www.sherrylwoods.com.

Winding River High School
Class of '91

Welcome Home——Ten Years Later
Do You Remember the Way We Were?

Gina Petrillo — Tastiest girl in the class. Elected most popular because nobody in town bakes a better double-chocolate brownie. Member of the Future Homemakers of America. Winner of three blue ribbons in the pie-baking contest and four in the cake-baking contest at the county fair.

Emma Rogers — That girl can swing...a bat, that is. Elected most likely to be the first female on the New York Yankees. Member of the Debate Club, the Honor Society and president of the senior class.

Lauren Winters — The girl with all the answers, otherwise known as the one you'd most like to be seated next to during an exam. Elected most likely to succeed. Class valedictorian. Member of the Honor Society, County Fair Junior Rodeo Queen and star of the junior and senior class plays.

Cassie Collins — Ringleader of the Calamity Janes. Elected most likely to land in jail. Best known for painting the town water tower a shocking pink and for making the entire faculty regret choosing teaching as a profession. Class record for detentions.

Karen (Phipps) Hanson — Better known as the Dreamer. Elected most likely to see the world. Member of the 4-H club, the Spanish and French clubs, and first-place winner at the county fair greased pig contest.

Prologue

The office at Café Tuscany on Manhattan's Upper West Side was little bigger than a broom closet, large enough for a desk, a chair and a bookshelf crammed with cookbooks, nutrition reports, menus and file boxes of handwritten recipes. It could only hold one person at a time, but at the moment Gina Petrillo's feeling of claustrophobia had more to do with the court document in her hand than the size of the space.

"I'm going to kill him," she muttered, fingers trembling as the summons to appear for a deposition slid to the desk. "If I ever get my hands on Bobby, I am going to kill him."

She had met Roberto Rinaldi when they were both studying cooking in Italy. A passionate enthusiast of fine food, Bobby was an intuitive genius in the kitchen. They had struck up an instant rapport that had more to do with ingenious blends of sauces and inventive uses for pasta than lust.

Truthfully, Gina wouldn't have trusted Bobby anywhere near her bed. The man was more fickle about women than he was about ingredients. He was constantly experimenting with both. He got away with it because he was charming, impossible to resist when he tempted with either delectable dishes or devilish kisses—at least according to his many conquests.

Gina had ignored his romantic overtures and concentrated on his skills in the kitchen. He was the most creative chef she had met during all of her studies, which was saying quite a lot. After forsaking college, she had studied at some of the finest culinary institutes in Europe. Though she had loved French cuisine, from the gourmet recipes of Paris to the simpler fare of Provence, Italian cooking spoke to her soul. Maybe it was genetic, maybe not, but the first time she had walked into the kitchen in Rome with its aromas of garlic, tomatoes and olive oil, she had felt at home.

It had been the same for Bobby, or so he had claimed. His recipes were both bold and adventurous. She doubted he'd ever tasted plain old pasta and tomato sauce, much less eaten canned ravioli, even as a child.

Five years ago, when the year-long course in Italy had ended, they had agreed to form a partnership, seek out investors among Bobby's financial contacts and open a restaurant in New York. It had taken another year to put the deal together, but it had been worth all of the scrimping and sacrifice, all of the long nights scraping paint and sanding floors. Café Tuscany had been a dream for both of them.

Apparently, it had also been Bobby's personal get-rich-quick scheme.

According to the summons she'd been handed an hour ago, Bobby had not only embezzled restaurant funds, but stolen from their backers, as well. A check of the café's account, made just minutes ago, confirmed the worst—the coffers were empty. And the rent was due, as were payments on invoices from most of their vendors.

Gina had no one to blame but herself for this disaster. She had allowed Bobby to keep track of their finances, because she was more interested in cooking and marketing than calculating. The fact that an outsider—an attorney representing the supposedly swindled backers—knew more about the state of the business's finances than she did was humiliating. It didn't seem to matter that she had done her part to make the business thrive. She was as much at fault as the man who'd run off with the money. At least, that was the implication in the summons.

Gina thought of all she had sacrificed to put Café Tuscany on the map, including a personal life. But it had been worth it. With a promotional push by one of her old high school classmates, superstar Lauren Winters, Gina had launched Café Tuscany as the hottest restaurant in a town where five-star dining and excellent neighborhood eateries were a dime a dozen. Prime tables were booked weeks in advance, and special events were sold out. Celebrities liked to be seen here, their presence always noted in the next day's papers. In the past year, their brand-new catering division had been booked for a dozen of society's most important charity events. With each success had come new bookings that kept her on the go morning till night.

So where had all that money gone? To finance some new scheme of Bobby's, no doubt. Or perhaps to freshen his designer wardrobe of Italian suits. Or maybe to buy diamonds for his latest lover. All Gina knew for certain was that none of it was in the bank, and that second notices for unpaid bills were stuffed into a drawer of the desk that Bobby had kept under lock and key. She'd broken into it an hour ago, right after she'd read through the damning words in the summons.

When she'd called Bobby's home—an expensive brownstone on the Upper East Side—she'd discovered that the line had been disconnected. His cell phone had gone unanswered. The man was gone.

The man was slime!

And because of him, this lawyer—she glanced at the summons again—this Rafe O'Donnell was on her trail, apparently convinced that she was in on the scheme, rather than another one of its victims.

Sitting there, stunned, Gina realized that her dream was not just ending, but crash landing. Unless she could come up with money—a lot of money—she would have to declare bankruptcy and close Café Tuscany within months, if not weeks. She might be able to stave off creditors for a while, but not indefinitely.

"I have to think," she muttered.

And she wasn't going to get the job done sitting in this closet. She needed fresh air and wide-open spaces. She needed to go home to Winding River, Wyoming.

She could leave the restaurant in the capable hands of her assistant manager for a week or so. She could call this O'Donnell person and postpone the deposition until, say, sometime in the next century.

With her high school class reunion in a few days, the timing couldn't be better. Her friends—the indomitable Calamity Janes—would be there to bolster her spirits. If she decided to ask, they would offer advice. Lauren would write a check on the spot to bail her out. Emma would give her expert legal counsel. And Karen and Cassie would find some way to make her laugh.

Gina sighed. They would do all of that and more *if* she decided to tell them just how badly she'd messed up.

In fact, she thought with the first bit of optimism she'd felt all day, they might even offer her a shotgun she could use if she ever spotted Roberto Rinaldi again.

Chapter One

"Gina Petrillo has gone *where?*" Rafe O'Donnell's head snapped up at his secretary's casual announcement.

"Wyoming. She called an hour ago and rescheduled the deposition," Lydia Allen repeated, looking entirely too cheerful.

If Rafe didn't know better he'd think she was glad that this Gina had escaped his clutches. He scowled at the woman who had been assigned to him when he'd first joined the firm, Whitfield, Mason and Lockhart, seven years earlier. At the time, she'd been with the firm for twenty years and claimed that she was always assigned to new recruits to make sure they were broken in properly. She was still with him because she swore that, to this day, he was too impossible to foist off on a less-seasoned secretary.

"Did I say it was okay to reschedule?" he inquired irritably.

"You've been in court all day," she said, clearly un-intimidated by his sharp tone. "We reschedule these things all the time."

"Not so some crook can go gallivanting off to Wyoming," he snapped.

"You don't know that Gina Petrillo is a crook," Lydia chided. "Innocent until proven guilty, remember?"

Rafe held on to his temper by a thread. "I do not need to be lectured on the principles of law by a grandmother," he said, deliberately minimizing whatever legal expertise she might legitimately consider her due.

Typically, she ignored the insult. "Maybe not, but you could use a few hard truths. I've eaten at that restaurant. So have most of the partners in this firm. If you weren't such a workaholic, you'd probably be a regular there, too. The food is fabulous. Gina Petrillo is a lovely, beautiful young woman. She is not a thief."

So, he thought, that explained the attitude. Lydia was personally acquainted with the elusive woman and dis-approved of Rafe's determination to link Gina Petrillo to her partner's crimes. As softhearted as his secretary was, she'd probably called Gina and warned her to get out of town.

"You say she's not a thief," he began with deceptive mildness in his best go-for-the-jugular mode. "Mind telling me how you reached that conclusion? Do you have a degree in psychology, perhaps? Access to the restaurant's books? Do you happen to have any evidence whatsoever that would actually exonerate her?"

"No, I do not have any evidence," she informed him with a huff. "Neither do you. But, unlike some people, I am a very good judge of character, Rafe O'Donnell."

Rafe was forced to concede that she was…usually.

"Now that Roberto," she continued, "I can believe he's stolen from people. He has shifty eyes."

"Thank you, Miss Marple," Rafe said snidely. "Roberto Rinaldi was not the only one with access to the money."

A good chunk of that money happened to belong to Rafe's socialite mother. She had been taken in by the man's charm. Rafe hadn't explored the exact nature of the relationship, but knowing his mother's track record, it hadn't been platonic. He was no more oblivious to his mother's faults than his father had been before the divorce, but he did his best to keep her from getting robbed blind.

"But Roberto is the one who's missing," Lydia pointed out. "He's the one you should be concentrating on."

"I would if I could find him," Rafe said, not bothering to hide his exasperation. "Which is one reason I want to talk to Gina Petrillo. She just might know where he is. Now, thanks to you, I don't even know where *she* is."

"Of course you do—I told you. She's gone to Wyoming."

"It's a big state. Care to narrow it down?"

She frowned at him. "There is no need to be sarcastic."

Rafe sighed. "Do you know where she is or not?"

"Of course I do."

"Then book me on the next flight."

"I doubt that Winding River has an airport. I'll check," she said, her expression unexpectedly brightening.

"Whatever," he said, not one bit happy about the images of Western wilderness that came to mind. "Just cancel everything on my calendar and get me out there by tomorrow night."

"Will do, boss. I'll go ahead and cancel everything through next week. You could use the time off."

Lydia's sudden eagerness, the spring in her step as she started to leave his office, had him frowning. "I don't need time off," he protested. "I'll take care of this over the weekend and be back here on Monday."

"Why don't you just play it by ear?"

His gaze narrowed. "What are you up to?"

"Just doing my job," she said with an innocent expression.

Rafe seriously doubted her innocence, but for the life of him he couldn't figure out why Lydia was so blasted anxious for him to jet off to Wyoming. She was not the kind of secretary who used the boss's absence to sneak out and shop or even to take long lunch hours. No, she was the kind who meddled, the kind who took great pride in making his private life a living hell with her well-meant pestering.

And she liked this Gina Petrillo, he thought, suddenly making the connection.

"Lydia!" he bellowed.

"You don't have to shout," she scolded. "I'm just outside the door."

"When you book my room in Winding River, make sure I'm all alone in it."

She feigned shock. "Why, of course I will."

"Don't look at me like that. It wouldn't be the first time some hotel mixup had me sharing a room with a woman you thought I ought to get to know better."

"I never—"

"Save it. Just make sure of it, Lydia, or you'll spend the rest of your career at Whitfield, Mason and Lockhart doing the filing."

She shot him an unrepentant grin. "I doubt that, sir. I know where all the bodies are buried."

Rafe sighed heavily. She did, too.

* * *

When the Winding River Wildcats did a class reunion, the festivities went on for three solid days. There was a welcome barbecue on Friday night, a rodeo during the day on Saturday, a dance Saturday night and a farewell picnic on Sunday. It all flowed right into the town's annual Fourth of July celebration.

Gina was less interested in all of that than she was in spending a few quiet hours with her oldest and dearest friends. For just a little while she wanted to forget all about that slime Roberto Rinaldi and the financial mess he'd left her to clean up.

"Couldn't we just go down to the Heartbreak, have a few beers, listen to some music and chill for a few hours?" she pleaded, even as the others were coaxing her off her parents' front porch and toward a car on Friday night.

"There will be beer and music at the barbecue," Emma told her. "Besides, since when have you ever turned down the chance to party? The only one in our crowd who was any wilder was Cassie."

At the mention of Cassie, Gina's spirits sank even lower. "I wish she'd come tonight."

"She's promised to be at the dance tomorrow night," Karen reminded her. "And you know perfectly well why she stayed away."

"Because of that run-in with Cole earlier," Gina said. "She really was shaken by that. He came within seconds of bumping face-to-face into their son."

"It might have been best if he had," Karen said. "I think she's just postponing the inevitable."

"Maybe so, but as much as I wish she were here, I am not going to let it spoil tonight," Lauren said. "Now, get moving, you guys. I've been living on lettuce a long time now. I haven't had a decent barbecue in years, and I am ready to pig out, no pun intended." She herded them toward the fancy sports utility vehicle she had rented for her visit.

Twenty minutes later Lauren turned into the parking lot at the school where they had shared some of the best times of their lives. Known far and wide as the Calamity Janes, the five of them had stirred up more trouble than any graduate before or since. Cassie had been the ringleader, but the rest of them had willingly gone along with whatever mischief she devised.

Now Karen lived on a ranch, Lauren was in Hollywood, Cassie was still struggling to keep her son a secret from his father and Emma was a hot-shot attorney in Denver. Like Emma and Lauren, Gina was considered one of the class success stories. The daughter of an insurance agent and a high school secretary, in high school Gina had earned much-needed spending money by working as a waitress right here in town. Now she owned her own very exclusive restaurant in New York. By anyone's standards, it was a rags-to-riches story.

If only they knew how close it was to turning around the other way, she thought with a sigh as they approached the football field that had been turned into giant picnic grounds for the night. A stage had been set up under the goal post at the north end, a pit for the roasted pig was at the opposite end and in between were rows of tables with every kind of food imaginable, all catered by the town's restaurants. Huge galvanized steel tubs were filled with ice and crammed with soft drinks and beer.

Classmates had already staked out spots for themselves by tossing blankets on the ground, but at the moment nobody was sitting. Everyone was milling around greeting people they hadn't seen since graduation ten years before.

Suddenly Gina felt an elbow being jammed into her ribs. "Hey," she protested, turning to face Lauren. "What was that for?"

The woman who had been declared most likely to succeed because of her brains, not her now-legendary beauty, gestured toward the bleachers, where a lone man sat, legs stretched out in front of him, elbows propped on the bench behind. He looked aloof and out of place. He also happened to be handsome as sin, but in the last few days Gina had sworn off the type. If she never met another sexy charmer, it would suit her just fine. In fact, at the moment, Bobby's disappearing act had made her view every male with healthy suspicion.

"Who, pray tell, is he?" Lauren asked. "He's definitely not one of us. Nobody we went to school with could improve that much in twenty years, much less ten."

Gina forced herself to give the stranger a closer inspection. True, he was gorgeous, in a citified, sophisticated way. Even in jeans and a chambray shirt—which looked brand-new from this distance—there was no mistaking the man for a cowboy. He was too polished, his chestnut hair a little too carefully trimmed, his complexion a little too pale, his cheekbones a little too aristocratic. He all but shouted that he was some Yankee blueblood.

"Well?" Lauren prodded. "Do you know him?"

Gina was certain she'd never seen him before, but that didn't seem to stop her heart from doing a little lurch or her stomach from taking a dip. It was possible he was someone's husband, sitting on the sidelines because he felt uncomfortable among all the strangers. She didn't think so, though. She had the uneasy sense that his penetrating gaze was locked directly on her. Not on Lauren, who tended to captivate any male in a room, but on her, Gina Petrillo, with the untamable hair, too-wide hips and a ten-year-old sundress she'd snagged from the back of the closet in her old bedroom.

Lauren, ever confident from years in the limelight, didn't seem to notice that the man's attention was elsewhere. She grinned at Gina. "Only one way to find out."

Gina wanted to tell her not to go over there, to steer as far away from the man as she could, but she knew the warning would only draw a hoot of laughter. There wasn't a person born who could intimidate Lauren once her curiosity was aroused. That confidence was something new. In high school Lauren had been as shy as she'd been brainy. The adoration of millions of fans had given her self-esteem a much-needed boost.

Gina deliberately turned her back on the scene and went in search of a desperately longed-for beer. She had just tipped up the can for a long, slow swallow when she heard Lauren say, "Oh, here you are. Gina, sweetie, this incredibly gorgeous man is looking for you. Aren't you lucky?"

Gina's stomach plummeted as she slowly turned to face them. With every fiber of her being she knew she wasn't the least bit lucky. Never had been, and certainly not lately. No, this man was not looking for her because he'd been dying to get her recipe for fettuccine.

"Gina Petrillo, Rafe O'Donnell," Lauren said, relinquishing him to Gina with a broad wink and then abandoning the two of them as if she'd just accomplished the matchmaking success of the century.

Gina recognized the name with a sense of inevitability. She forced herself to look straight into the man's unreadable topaz eyes. There was little point in pretending that she didn't recognize the name. Nor did she have to work very hard to figure out what he was doing here. She was not going to let him rattle her, though. She would remain cool, calm and collected if it killed her. She refused to let him think for a second that she was harboring any sense of guilt.

"A long way from home, aren't you, Mr. O'Donnell?"

"As are you, Ms. Petrillo."

"No, this *is* my home," she said firmly.

"And New York?"

"Where I work."

"Not any longer, if I have anything to say about it."

She gave him a wry look. "Then I guess the battle lines are drawn. It's a good thing you're not either judge or jury. I might be quaking in my boots."

"You should be, anyway. I'm very good at what I do."

"And what is it that you do, Mr. O'Donnell? Condemn people without a trial?"

"Get at the facts, Ms. Petrillo. That was the whole purpose of that deposition you skipped out on."

She regarded him with indignation. "I didn't skip out on anything. Check your appointment book. I rescheduled."

"Without my permission."

"Your secretary didn't seem to have a problem with it."

"Yes, well, Lydia sometimes forgets who's in charge."

If it had been anyone else under any other circumstance, Gina might have grinned at his resigned expression. Instead, she said only, "You must find that extremely annoying."

"Mostly it's just an inconvenience," he corrected.

"Yes, I imagine chasing halfway across the country after bad guys like me must play havoc with your schedule."

To her surprise, he chuckled.

"You have no idea," he said. "I had really big plans for this weekend."

"Oh? A ball game with the kids? Maybe a charity event with the wife?"

"No kids. No wife."

That news set off totally inappropriate little butterflies in Gina's stomach. To her deep regret they seemed to be doing a victory dance. She refused to let him see that he could disconcert her in the slightest way—especially not in *that* way.

She studied him thoughtfully. "A hot date, then?"

"Nope."

"Surely you weren't spending the weekend all alone, Mr. O'Donnell."

"Afraid so. Of course, I would have had my share of entertainment. Before I left I got a subpoena for the Café Tuscany books. I had someone pick them up yesterday morning. I understand your assistant was very helpful. Too bad you and your partner aren't that cooperative. Where can I find Rinaldi, by the way?"

Gina barely contained a groan. *That* explained the frantic messages she'd been getting from Deidre all day. Gina hadn't called back because she had vowed to take this weekend off from everything connected to the restaurant. She had figured Monday would be soon enough to return the call and face whatever catastrophe had struck. Just one more bad decision she would have to live with. They were stacking up faster than the ones the Calamity Janes had made in high school.

"I'm sure those books would have been as illuminating as anything I can tell you," she said. "You should have stayed at home with them. You could have crunched numbers all weekend long. As for Bobby, if you locate him, let me know. I have a few choice words I'd like to share with him.''

"Do you expect me to believe he skipped out without telling you?"

"Frankly, I don't care what you believe. Now, go home, Mr. O'Donnell. It's not too late to cozy up with those financial records. Why not fly back tonight?"

"Because I gave the pilot on the charter jet that brought me here from Denver the night off and I hate to ruin his evening," the attorney countered. "He was looking forward to doing some line dancing at someplace called the Heartbreak."

"How very thoughtful of you. And how very expensive to go around chartering jets to get from here to there. Do your clients know how you toss their money around?"

"Oh, this trip's on me," he said easily. He glanced around at the crowded field, took a deliberate sniff of the smoky, barbecue-scented air. "I haven't been to an event like this in a long time."

She regarded him with skepticism. "For such a proponent of truth, Mr. O'Donnell, that's quite a fib. You've *never* been to an event like this, have you?"

She deliberately looked him over from head to toe. "I'm guessing some East Coast prep school, then Harvard. If you've ever been to a reunion, I'm sure it was in some fancy hotel or private country club. And my hunch is that the closest you've ever come to a horse is on a New York street corner and there was a cop mounted on its back."

"You'd be wrong," he said without rancor. "I went to public schools, then to Yale, not Harvard."

"That's not exactly a significant distinction."

"I suggest you not say that to an alumnus of either

university. We do like to cling to our illusions of supremacy.''

"Well, cling all you like, just do it somewhere else. I'm here to have a good time with some old friends. I don't want to find you lurking in the shadows everywhere I turn."

"Too bad. I'm not going anywhere."

His vehemence was annoying, but not all that surprising. "What really brought you running all the way out here?" she asked curiously. "Are you afraid I'm going to disappear? Are you hoping to discover I've stashed the missing money in a mattress at my parents' house?''

The idea seemed to intrigue him. "Have you?"

"Nope. No stash. No hiding place. And I can show you my airline ticket. It's round-trip. Go home, Mr. O'Donnell. I'll see you right on schedule in a couple of weeks.''

"We could get this out of the way right here and now," he suggested. "Then I could get back to New York and you could enjoy the rest of your weekend."

"Without an attorney present? I don't think so."

He shrugged. "Then I guess you'll just have to get used to having me underfoot for…how long did you say you were planning to stay?''

"Two weeks."

The news seemed to make him very unhappy, but he nodded. "Two weeks, then. I'll look forward to it."

Gina sighed. "Suit yourself. I'm going to get another beer."

He seemed to find that amusing. "Drinking won't make you forget I'm here."

"No, I imagine it won't," she agreed. "It would take a blow on the head to accomplish that. But the beer might make your presence more palatable."

She gave him a jaunty salute. "See you in court, Mr. O'Donnell."

"Oh, I'll be seeing you long before that," he said smoothly. "In fact, I'll be everywhere you turn."

If only his mission weren't to put her in jail, Gina thought with a trace of wistfulness, she might actually look forward to that.

As it was, the knot of dread in her stomach tightened. She might not be guilty of anything except the bad judgment to go into business with Bobby, but Rafe O'Donnell struck her as the kind of man who could dig up secrets, twist words and paint a very dark picture of the saintliest person on earth.

And he intended to stay right here in Winding River turning over rocks, no doubt, looking for incriminating evidence, pestering her friends. She shuddered at the prospect.

Maybe she should just get it over with. Talk to him, and send him on his way. But that idea held no appeal, either. She needed time to gather her thoughts and see an attorney back in New York. She didn't want to drag Emma or anyone else here into this unless she absolutely had to. It was her disaster and she would fix it. Assuming it could be fixed.

In the meantime the music had started and nobody loved dancing more than Gina did. She could postpone that beer for a few more minutes. She gave Rafe O'Donnell a considering look.

"Can you do a two-step?" she asked.

He looked at her blankly. "What's that?"

She regarded him with pity. "Never mind," she said, reaching for his hand. "Just follow my lead."

He caught on more quickly than she had expected. He

wasn't good, but he wasn't tripping over his own feet or stepping on her's, either.

"You do rise to a challenge, don't you?" she teased.

"There's very little I won't do to win," he agreed solemnly.

"Are we still talking about dancing?"

"Were we ever?"

Gina sighed. So that was the way it was going to be. He was never going to let her forget why he was here.

"I think I'll have that beer after all," she said, even before the music ended. She started away, then turned back. "Leave my friends out of this."

"I won't say anything," he agreed, then had to ruin it by adding, "For the time being."

"Look, Mr. O'Donnell…"

"I think since we're going to become so well acquainted over the next couple of weeks, you should call me Rafe."

She shrugged off the request. "Whatever. The point is, they don't know anything about this and I don't want them to."

"Why? Your friend Lauren makes ten million a movie. She could write you a check and put an end to this right now. You could pay off all those people who've been bilked, settle up the restaurant's accounts and life would go on. You'd never have to see me again."

"She could," Gina agreed. "But it's not her problem. It's mine." She leveled a look straight into his eyes. "No, let me correct that. It's Bobby's."

"But he left you holding the bag, didn't he?"

She held up her hands. "I'm not doing this. Not now. Good night, Mr. O'Donnell."

She deliberately turned her back on him and walked away, but with every step she took, she felt his gaze burning into her. She was glad he couldn't see her face, because then he'd know exactly how badly the encounter had shaken her.

Halfway across the field, she ran into Lauren.

"What did you do with that gorgeous man?"

"That gorgeous man is a viper," Gina snapped.

Instantly her friend's teasing expression faded. "What did he do?" Lauren demanded, her gaze searching the field for the man who'd offended her friend.

Gina grinned. "It's okay. Settle down. It's nothing I can't deal with."

"Are you sure?"

"Absolutely."

But even though she managed to inject a note of confidence into her voice for Lauren's sake, Gina couldn't help wondering if Rafe O'Donnell wasn't way more than she could handle. She thought of the way her pulse had skipped in his presence, then amended the thought: he might be more than she could handle in more ways than one.

Chapter Two

Rafe had been stunned when he'd realized that the woman sashaying over to him earlier in the evening was *the* Lauren Winters, an actress renowned for her beauty and her box office appeal. Who would have imagined finding such a glamorous superstar in a one-horse town in the middle of nowhere? To top it off, she seemed to fit right in. No one was gawking. No one was begging for autographs. Clearly she wasn't just a celebrity imported for the event, but a hometown girl.

But as intrigued as he was to be face-to-face with the superstar, he'd barely been able to pull his gaze away from her friend. From the moment Lauren had introduced him to Gina, he'd been captivated. That was the only word for it, and it was damned inconvenient. He didn't trust her. He didn't like her. But his body didn't seem to give two hoots about any of that.

Gina Petrillo was tall and slender with black eyes and

dark hair that curled to her shoulders in sexy disarray. There was an earthy quality to her that reminded him of some of the most legendary Italian beauties. He could instantly envision her standing over a steaming pot of tomato sauce and just as easily imagine her in his bed, in a steamy tangle of arms and legs. He couldn't think of the last time he'd reacted on such a purely male level to a woman.

Of course, the fact that she was a thief—okay, an alleged thief, he conceded, thinking of Lydia's admonition—took a little of the fun away from the discovery that he was attracted to her. He had a feeling he was going to spend a lot of time reminding himself that Gina Petrillo was trouble. He would probably spend even more time in cold showers.

Holding her for that dance, watching the sway of her hips as she'd walked away from him, he'd found himself regretting the fact that she was so thoroughly forbidden. Then, again, maybe that was the real allure.

And not only was she forbidden, she didn't seem to trust him any more than he did her. That offended him. Most people considered him solid and reliable. In fact, he was one of the most respected attorneys at a firm that prided itself on its respectability. In some circles he was even considered a prize catch.

Not that he was any sort of playboy, but he was used to women being eager to see him. He seldom had time for even half the women who called asking him to accompany them to social functions. He had a hunch it would be a cold day in hell before Gina asked him to dance again, much less to join her for dinner. That made her a challenge, and as she had already guessed, he loved a challenge.

The smart thing would be to speak to a local judge,

arrange a quick deposition—first thing tomorrow morning, if possible—and then hightail it out of town before
he lost sight of his professional ethics.

The only problem with that was that it would leave
Gina Petrillo on her own in Wyoming. She'd be able to
sneak off to who-knew-where the minute his back was
turned. And she was his best link to Roberto Rinaldi. The
deposition was only half of what he wanted from her. He
also wanted her to lead him to that sleazebag partner of
hers. Sooner or later she was going to make contact with
the man, if only to strangle him herself...or to get her
share of the cash he'd stolen.

No, he concluded, he was here to stay. At least until
Gina went back to New York, which she'd insisted would
be in two weeks.

Two endless weeks, he thought despondently. Lydia
would be elated.

He listened to the annoying whine of a fiddle as the
band tuned up for yet another round of country songs, and
shuddered. Why couldn't the woman have run off to Italy?
Or Paris? Or anyplace civilized where the music tended
to be classical?

"Care to dance, Mr. O'Donnell?"

He gazed down into Lauren's crystal-blue eyes and
wondered why he wasn't the least bit tempted by the superstar. Because the only eyes on his mind were black as
onyx and belonged to a woman who was off-limits, he
made himself nod.

"I'd be honored," he told her. If nothing else, it would
be a story to tell when he got back home. Maybe even to
repeat to his children, if he ever got around to marrying.

They had taken only a few awkward steps to the unfamiliar rhythm when Lauren came to a stop and dropped

any pretense of friendliness. "You don't know much about the Texas two-step, do you, Mr. O'Donnell?"

"Can't say that I do," he admitted. "Tonight is the first time I've tried it."

"Do you consider yourself a quick learner?" she asked.

He regarded her warily. "Under most circumstances."

"Okay, then, here's another lesson," she said. "You don't know any more about Gina than you do about the two-step. She won't tell me why you're here, but your presence is clearly upsetting her, and I don't like that. She's a terrific person and she's among friends, Mr. O'Donnell. You tangle with her, you tangle with all of us."

He grinned at the feisty defense and the warning. "I'll keep that in mind."

"I'm not saying that for your amusement," she snapped. "I mean it. People who underestimate me live to regret it."

He managed a more somber expression. "I'm aware of that, Ms. Winters. You've made your point."

She studied him intently, then nodded, evidently satisfied. "See that you don't forget it."

He watched as she went back to a cluster of three women, Gina among them. Lauren gave her friend a fierce hug, a public demonstration of support meant for his benefit, no doubt. He admired the show of loyalty, but it didn't change his mind about Gina.

Whether Gina was a thief or not remained to be seen, but her partner was, and that made her guilty of very bad judgment if nothing else. Nothing she'd said or done tonight had persuaded him of her innocence. In fact, quite the opposite.

The way he saw it, Gina was even more dangerous than he'd anticipated. She was savvy and unpredictable. She had a smart mouth. With her restaurant under siege, she just might get it into her head that she had nothing to lose. She could decide to run. And she was surrounded by people who evidently would do just about anything to protect her no matter how guilty she might be.

He was going to have to keep a clear head, which was doubly difficult given the effect she had on him. Obviously, what he needed was a good night's sleep, though he doubted he'd get it with Gina's sexy image plaguing him. He glanced around until he found her in the crowd.

She was dancing again, head thrown back, her gaze locked with some cowboy's. Rafe felt his blood boil. He wanted to stride across the field and yank her out of the man's embrace. The depth of that unexpected and unfamiliar streak of jealousy startled him. He hadn't cared enough about any woman to be jealous, not ever. This was not good, not good at all.

He definitely needed to get back to his motel room, alone, and get his sex-starved emotions under control. He hadn't mentioned to Gina that he'd brought the Café Tuscany books with him. Studying those cold, hard figures ought to put things back into perspective. And they were a whole lot more reliable and easier to understand than any woman. His mother had taught him that.

Gina didn't get a wink of sleep all night long. Despite her cool responses and bravado the night before, Rafe O'Donnell had gotten to her. She knew all about the fancy Park Avenue law firm he worked for. She'd recognized the name from its frequent mentions on the news, and some of the partners were among her best customers. They didn't take cases they didn't intend to win. She didn't doubt that he was as driven and determined as the rest of them.

Which meant he was going to make her life a living hell. Oh, in the end, she might be able to prove that Bobby had acted alone, but not without paying a high price. Her reputation would be tarnished. Between unpaid bills and legal fees, the restaurant would be forced to close. And she'd be right back where she started five years ago, working in somebody else's kitchen to scrape up enough money to open her own restaurant.

It would take longer this time, too, because she wouldn't have Bobby to draw in investors. In fact, her link to Bobby would probably prevent anyone except the most foolhardy from lending her a dime.

Sighing, she crawled out of bed, pulled on a pair of faded jeans, a short-sleeved blouse and the cowboy boots she hadn't worn since she'd left Winding River ten years ago. They still fit perfectly. Maybe there was a message there, that Winding River was where she really belonged, where people still felt a shred of respect for her.

Her parents had long since left the house. Her father worked Saturdays. Her mother spent the morning with the altar guild at church and her afternoon doing errands. Gina was used to late nights and sleeping in. She'd gotten to bed before midnight the night before, but add in a little jet lag and her schedule was completely upside down. It felt like noon, which it was in New York. The clock said otherwise.

She poured herself a cup of coffee, made two slices of toast from her mother's homemade sourdough bread, then went onto the porch. It was already hot outside, better suited for iced tea than coffee, but she drank it anyway. Maybe a jolt of caffeine would help her think more clearly so she could decide what to do about Rafe O'Donnell.

Unfortunately, the only ideas that came to mind had more to do with discovering what his mouth would feel like against her own than they did with getting him out of town.

Too restless to sit still, she grabbed the keys to her mother's car, which had been left for her, and headed for town. She parked in the middle of the block on Main Street and considered her options. She could go to Stella's and probably find a half dozen people she knew who'd be glad to chat with her over another cup of coffee. Or she could go to the Italian restaurant down the block, where Tony would probably let her work off her frustrations over his stove.

No contest, she thought, with a stirring of anticipation.

Tony Falcone had been her mentor. He'd hired her as a waitress while she was still in high school, but it hadn't been long before he'd discovered that her real talent was in the kitchen. He'd taught her to make lasagna and spaghetti sauce with meatballs. He'd let her experiment with new recipes when cooking the traditional dishes had grown boring. And then he had helped her to persuade her parents that she would be better off going to culinary schools around the world than to any traditional college. It had been a tough sell, especially to her father, who'd been convinced that a degree in accounting would be a lot more practical. Given her current circumstances, Gina had to admit her father might have had a point.

A wave of nostalgia washed over her as she approached the back door at Tony's and knocked, then opened it without waiting for a response from inside.

"Anybody in here have a good recipe for meatballs?" she called out.

"Cara mia," Tony said, a smile spreading across his round face when he saw her. "Where have you been? I heard you were coming home, but then nothing. I am

insulted that I was not at least the second stop on your list after your parents."

"I know, I know," she said, giving him a kiss on the cheek. "Will you forgive me?"

He studied her. "That depends."

"On?"

"How long you intend to stay. It has been too long, Gina. My customers are grumbling about the same old food, week after week. Not a day goes by that someone doesn't ask when you will be back to liven up the menu."

"What do you tell them?"

"That you are now a famous chef in New York, and that if they want to eat your food, they will have to travel there."

Gina eyed with longing the huge old stove with its simmering pots. "I could fix something for tonight," she offered. "Maybe a spicy penne *arrabiata* or a Greek-style pizza with black olives and feta cheese."

"But you are on vacation," Tony protested. "I cannot ask you to cook."

"You didn't ask. I offered. Besides, I have some thinking to do, and I always think more clearly as I cook."

He studied her intently. "Problems, *cara mia?* Do you want to talk about them? I may not be able to solve them, but I can listen. Sometimes that is all we need, yes? An objective listener while we sort through things?"

Gina debated telling Tony everything. She knew he would keep it to himself. She also knew he would sympathize with her predicament because he, more than anyone, knew how important her restaurant was to her.

"Are you sure you wouldn't mind?" she asked.

He regarded her with feigned indignation. "How many nights did I listen to you go on and on about this boyfriend or that?"

She grinned ruefully. "More than I care to think about, but this is different."

"How?"

"Because it really matters."

"When you were sixteen, those boys mattered, too."

She thought back to the string of broken hearts she'd suffered. "Okay, you're right. I guess it's all a matter of perspective, isn't it?"

"I will fix us both an espresso and we will talk." He gestured toward the front. "Go in there and sit."

"But you have things to do," she protested. "We can talk here."

"Nothing that can't wait. Now, go. I will be there in a minute."

Gina walked into the dining room with its familiar red-checked tablecloths, the dripping candles stuck in old Chianti bottles, the wide-planked oak floor and the big picture window overlooking Main Street. An inexpertly done mural of Naples had been painted on one wall by Tony's homesick wife, Francesca.

By comparison, Café Tuscany had five-star ambience, but Gina felt perfectly at home here with the rich scents drifting from the kitchen and the sunlight spilling in the window. An astonishing sense of peace crept over her. Right here, right now, she could believe everything would be all right.

Tony joined her at a table in front. She smiled as she accepted the cup of dark espresso and took her first sip. "Still the best," she told him. "I grind and blend my own beans, but it's not the same."

"When I die, I will leave you the secret in my will," he teased. "Now talk to me. What is this big trouble in your life?"

Gina sighed and gazed into Tony's dark-brown eyes.

There was so much fatherly concern there. She realized suddenly just how much she had missed this man, missed sitting here and talking about her hopes and dreams until she was certain he must be bored silly, but he had never complained. Some of the time Francesca had been with them, clucking over Gina's disappointments and offering encouragement.

"Did I ever thank you for everything you did for me?" she asked.

"You did, but there was no need. For Francesca and me, you are the daughter we never had."

"How is Francesca? I should have asked."

"Still the most beautiful woman in the world," he said, a gleam in his eyes. "She will be here soon. It will make her very happy to see you again. You can tell her everything you saw in Italy. She still dreams of seeing it again one day."

"Then take her, Tony," she said with a sudden sense of urgency. "Don't let time slip away."

He regarded her worriedly. "You aren't sick, are you?"

"No, no, of course not."

"It's just that you sounded so sad, as if there were things you wanted that you might never have."

She shook her head. "No, just things that mean the world to me that I could lose." She told him the whole story then, leaving out none of the sordid details about Bobby's betrayal of her and their investors.

True to his word, Tony listened and said nothing until she wound down. "Now, to top it off, the attorney who's filed charges against Bobby is right here in Winding River. He thinks I'm as guilty as Bobby or, at the very least, that I know something that will help his case," she concluded.

"But you don't?"

She shook her head. "I was as shocked as anyone. I'm embarrassed to say that the first clue I had of how bad things are came when I read that deposition. That's when I looked at the books."

"Then tell him that, tell this man what you have told me. Hold nothing back. He will believe you." He patted her hand. "If he does not, send him to me. I will tell him that Gina Petrillo does not lie."

If only it were that simple, Gina thought. She glanced outside and spotted Rafe standing on the sidewalk, leaning against the bumper of a very fancy car, staring right back at her.

"Speak of the devil," she muttered, resigned to the fact that the man was going to be true to his word and haunt her everywhere she went, even here in this place that had always been her sanctuary.

Tony followed her gaze. "That is Rafe O'Donnell?"

"In the flesh."

"He looks like a reasonable man."

"He's not," Gina said. "If he were, he would go away and leave me alone. I told him when I would return to New York. He doesn't believe me. He's determined to stick to me like glue until I go back."

Tony stood up. "Then we should invite him in to join us, show him that you have nothing to hide, nothing to fear from him."

"I don't know," Gina protested, but Tony was already opening the door and beckoning Rafe inside.

"Better you should sit here than loiter on the sidewalk outside," Tony told him, ushering him to the table. "I will bring you an espresso, then I must get back to work in the kitchen so things will be ready for lunch."

Rafe sat down opposite Gina, his long legs stretched out in front of him. He looked totally at ease, not one bit like a man on a mission to make her life a living hell. And, to her very deep regret, he was still the sexiest male she'd stumbled across in a very long time. She had really, really hoped she'd been wrong about that.

Rafe glanced around, surveying the restaurant with fascination.

"Is this where you got your start?" he asked.

"I worked at Stella's for a while as a waitress, then came here. Tony taught me to cook."

Rafe gestured toward the mural. "Who's the artist?"

Gina turned to look at the familiar painting, tried to imagine how it must look through Rafe's no-doubt jaded eyes.

"Francesca, Tony's wife, painted it from an old photograph," she explained a bit defensively. "She was born in Naples. She says that painting keeps her from being homesick, so I suggest you not make fun of it."

"Why would I do that?"

"Because it's probably too hokey for a sophisticated man like you," she said.

"Are you sure you're not projecting? I like it."

She studied him to see if he was mocking her, but his expression was serious. "You really like it?" she asked skeptically.

"I said I did, didn't I? I'm not an art snob, Gina." He regarded her pointedly. "Are you?"

She flushed at the accusation. "I always loved it because of what it meant to Francesca, but it's not exactly great art."

"It doesn't need to be. There's a simplicity to it that I find appealing. It gives the restaurant a personal touch, a certain charm." He met her gaze evenly. "Now I imagine your restaurant has Venetian-glass chandeliers, oil paintings you picked up in Florence, dark wood, fresh flowers and green linen tablecloths.''

He was closer to the truth than Gina cared to admit. Bobby had believed that to charge the outrageous prices he intended to charge, the atmosphere had to be elegant.

"Have you been to Café Tuscany?" she asked.

"Nope."

"Then you shouldn't be making judgments."

"Which must mean I got it exactly right," he said, grinning.

"You did not."

"Which part was wrong?"

"The tablecloths are dark red," she murmured.

His grin spread. "What was that? I don't think I heard you."

"Oh, get over yourself," she said, this time very clearly. "I have to go."

"I haven't even had my espresso yet," he chided her.

"Then, by all means, stay and enjoy it. I'm sure Tony will be glad to keep you company."

Casting one last wistful look toward the kitchen, Rafe rose to his feet. "Unfortunately, it's not his company I'm after. Where you go, I go, so lead on, Gina."

She scowled at him. "You're serious, aren't you? You're going to tail me like you would some common criminal?"

"Oh, I doubt there's anything common about you," he said, but he didn't deny his intentions. "You could save me some trouble and just invite me along."

"The very last thing I want to do is save you from putting yourself out. If you want to follow me, then I suggest you get into that fancy car of yours and rev the engine, because I don't slow down to wait for anybody."

He regarded her with a resigned expression. "Suit yourself. Do your worst, Gina. I promise I'll keep up. And just in case you have any ideas about exceeding the speed limit to lose me, remember I have my cell phone with me and I'll use it to call the sheriff."

"The sheriff is a friend of mine," she countered.

"Which won't matter when I suggest to him that you skipped out on a court-ordered deposition."

"I did not skip out," she said, her voice rising. "I postponed it. You know that."

"Do I?" he asked innocently. "I imagine by the time we get it all sorted out, you'll be late for whatever it is you're so anxious to get to."

Gina held on to her temper by a very slender thread. "I am not anxious to get anywhere except away from you," she said, gritting her teeth. "Oh, never mind. My car's down the block. You might as well come with me. I'm going to a rodeo. It might be interesting to see how you take to all that hot air and dust."

"If you want to see me sweat, I can think of far more interesting ways to go about it," Rafe taunted.

Gina felt her skin burn. Wasn't it bad enough that the man was out to torment her over the mess Bobby had created? Now he apparently intended to drive her crazy with sexual innuendoes that stirred her imagination in ways destined to leave her hot and bothered and thoroughly frustrated.

"Don't even go there," she warned him tightly. "You're probably breaking at least a dozen different rules of ethics just by hinting at such a thing."

"At least that many," he agreed, as if it were of no importance. His gaze locked with hers. "But something tells me it might be worth it."

Judging from the way her heart was thundering in her chest, Gina was very much afraid he could be right about that.

Chapter Three

It had only been twenty-four hours since his arrival, and already Rafe was having a really hard time remembering why he had come to Winding River. For a man known for his razor-sharp mind and powers of concentration, it was a disconcerting experience. He'd certainly never had any trouble in the past when it came to focusing on the best interests of his clients.

Now, however, he couldn't seem to take his eyes off the woman sitting beside him in the stands at the rodeo arena. That was truly saying something, given the level of activity going on in the center of the ring and the cheers sounding all around him. His mind was drifting in all sorts of wicked directions, just as it had the night before.

Okay, he told himself, all that proved was that he was a healthy, virile male who'd been without intimate female companionship for way too long. Whose mind wouldn't wander just a bit around a woman like Gina? Pleased with the assessment of his state of mind as being perfectly normal, he gave himself permission to study her even more intently.

Gina's dark-eyed gaze was fixed on the current bronc rider with total absorption. Her cheeks were bright. Her hair, which was caught up in a red and white bandanna, had surprising auburn highlights in it. At the moment, as some man she apparently knew tried to stay on the back of a particularly wild horse, she appeared to be holding her breath. When time ran out and he was still solidly in the saddle, her cheer almost deafened Rafe. Eyes shining, she faced him.

"Did you see that? He did it. That's the toughest horse in the competition and Randy stayed with him. Amazing."

"Amazing," Rafe echoed, but his comment had nothing to do with the winning rider.

Her gaze narrowed. "Are you even paying attention?"

"Absolutely. Your friend won."

"He's leading, at any rate. There's another round of competition," she said, excitement still shining in her eyes.

It was the most unguarded she had been around Rafe since they'd met. Seeing her like that, filled with enthusiasm, her expression open, laughter glinting in her eyes, made him want things that were impossible. It had probably been safer all the way around when she'd kept him at a cool distance. The temptation to kiss her was almost too much to resist.

"Want something cold to drink?" he asked, needing to put some space between them. Being in a state of semi-arousal for the past hour was beginning to get to him.

She feigned exaggerated shock. "You're willing to go off and leave me here all alone for a few minutes? Are you sure you trust me not to steal the wildest horse in the stables and flee over the Canadian border?''

"Actually, no, but since the horses are otherwise engaged and I have the car keys, I'm not nearly as worried about it as I might be if the circumstances were different." He was still rather proud of the way he'd managed to get those keys away from her and into his own pocket.

"How do you know I don't have a spare set?" she retorted.

He gazed directly into her eyes, a look he'd perfected in the courtroom. It commanded total honesty. "Do you?"

She hesitated, then sighed. "No. And just for the record, I resent like crazy the fact that you manipulated those keys out of my possession."

He grinned. "I didn't wrestle you for them, Gina. You handed them over so I could drive."

"Right, after you gave me some very sincere hogwash about how you'd been just dying to test-drive a car like my mother's."

"You bought it, didn't you?"

"Long enough for you to get behind the wheel," she agreed. "Then I remembered that my mother's car is a very nondescript Chevy with eighty thousand miles on it."

"And what I told you was the absolute truth," Rafe insisted. "I've never driven anything like it."

Gina rolled her eyes. "Yes, *that* I can believe."

He chuckled. "Do you want something to drink or not?"

"A soda," she said finally, fanning herself with the program. "Orange, if they have it."

The action only drew attention to the perspiration beaded on her chest. Rafe's gaze seemed to be riveted to the exposed skin. He swallowed hard and resisted the urge to nab that program and use it to cool off his own over-heated flesh.

"Lots of ice," she added. "I'm sweltering out here."

"Want to come with me?" he asked, forgetting all about his intention to give himself a break from her non-stop assault on his senses. "Maybe we can find some shade somewhere and cool off."

She seemed to debate that, then finally nodded. "Let's go."

Rafe let her lead the way to the refreshment stand, or-dered large sodas for both of them, then glanced around until he spotted a spreading cottonwood tree with a patch of shade beneath.

"Over there okay?" he asked.

"Perfect," Gina agreed.

Seemingly oblivious to the fact that the ground was more dirt than grass, she sank down, accepted her drink, then sighed. "This is heaven," she murmured. She snagged an ice cube from the drink, held it at the base of her throat and let it slowly melt. The water trickled across her flushed skin, then ran between her breasts.

As he watched her, Rafe's throat went dry as a parched desert. Not even a long, slow swallow of his drink had a cooling effect. He was beginning to regret inviting Gina to leave the stands with him. Hell, he regretted accom-panying her to the rodeo in the first place. It was testing him to his limits to keep his hands to himself.

He could have been in a nice, air-conditioned motel room, a beer in his hand, and all those damning Café Tuscany figures right in front of him. That's where he ought to be, not out here on the verge of sunstroke and filled with more lust than he'd felt in the past twelve months combined, all directed at a woman who was totally untrustworthy, perhaps even more so than his own mother.

"Something wrong?" she inquired.

Her expression was all innocence as she let another ice cube melt, holding it a little lower, a little more provocatively this time. She'd stripped off her blouse when they'd first arrived, giving him a bad moment or two before he'd realized that she was wearing a tank top beneath. Between her deliberately provocative actions with that ice and the perspiration, the already revealing tank top was damp and clinging in a way that left very little to Rafe's overheated imagination.

"Not a thing," he claimed. "Why?"

"You look a little flushed."

"Is that so surprising? It must be ninety-five degrees out here."

"But it's a dry heat," she countered.

"Heat is heat."

Pure mischief lit her eyes. "I could help you cool off," she offered.

Before he could respond or guess what she intended, she upended her drink over his head. Fortunately, it was mostly water and melting ice by now, but the splash of frigid liquid against his burning skin was a shock.

Gina was already up and dancing away by the time he caught his breath. Rafe was on his feet in a heartbeat, fighting indignation and—to his own surprise—laughter.

"You are in such trouble," he said.

"Mighty tough words from a man who's dripping wet," she taunted. "I did you a favor. Try to keep that in mind."

"Oh, I have no intention of forgetting what you did," he said, regarding her with a deceptively lazy look as he halted his pursuit.

He waited until she stopped backing nervously away, gave her time to grow complacent, then moved so quickly she didn't have time to react. He snagged her wrist and hauled her into his arms.

He captured her gasp with his first kiss, then settled in to discover exactly how she tasted, exactly how her lips felt beneath his. There was a lingering sweet taste of orange soda to her mouth, a willing pliancy to her lush lips.

Her body fit against his as if they'd been made for each other. Between the dousing his clothes had taken, the dampness of hers and the skyrocketing heat of that kiss, he was surprised they weren't enveloped in steam.

It took a very long time—too long, by his own rigid standard of ethics—for him to discover everything he'd wanted to know about the taste and texture of her mouth. He released her suddenly and with tremendous reluctance, muttering a curse under his breath.

Wide-eyed and open-mouthed, she stared at him for a full minute and then the heat rose in her cheeks right along with a flash of temper in her eyes.

"You had no right to do that," she snapped.

"No," he said mildly. "You're right. I didn't. I'm sorry. It was a mistake."

His admission and his apology seemed to throw her off stride.

"If you think that's good enough to make me forget what just happened here, you're crazy."

Despite himself, he chuckled at that. "Yes, I imagine it will take a good deal more to make me forget it, too."

"That is not what I meant, and you know it," she said with a scowl.

"Okay, let's take a step back and reassess what just happened," he suggested reasonably.

"Oh, don't use that lawyerly tone with me. We both know what happened. You kissed me."

"You provoked me."

"I dumped water on you. If anything, that should have cooled off your libido, not inflamed it."

He shrugged. "What can I say? I obviously have a perverse streak."

"How about saying 'I'm sorry, it will never happen again,'" she suggested.

"I've already apologized." He met her gaze. "And sadly I *can't* promise it will never happen again."

"You have to," she said, sounding a little desperate.

"Why?"

"Because it's the right thing to do, because you have no business kissing me, because I have no business kissing you." She frowned at him. "You think I'm a criminal, for heaven's sake. Are you beginning to get the picture?"

Unfortunately, Rafe was, though he doubted it was the same picture she was getting. The one in his mind had him carting her straight off to bed to finish what they'd started. Given his belief that she was a thief, he figured that was a really, really lousy idea...and way too tempting at the moment. His very recent lapse in judgment was proof enough he couldn't be trusted within fifty feet of her.

He reached in his pocket, took out her car keys and tossed them to her. She regarded him with surprise.

"How are you getting back to town?" she asked.

"The old-fashioned way," he said, turning his back on her and striding away.

"Rafe, you can't walk all the way back," she protested, chasing after him. "You'll die of heat stroke."

"Thanks for your concern, but I'll be fine."

"You will not be fine. Don't be stubborn. I'll drive you back."

He faced her. "How do I know you won't try to ravish me the second we get to my motel?"

She gave him a wry look. "Oh, I think I can pretty well guarantee that you're safe."

He shrugged. "Okay, then, I trust you."

She regarded him skeptically. "Oh, really?"

"About that, anyway." He tapped a finger against the sunburned tip of her nose. "We'll have to see about the rest. I'll think it over while I'm walking."

"I don't suppose you could keep on going all the way back to New York and ponder the evidence there?" she asked wistfully.

"Not a chance."

Gina heaved a resigned sigh. "Yeah, that's what I figured."

That blistering, mind-boggling kiss was still very much on Gina's mind when she walked into the high school gym that night for the reunion dance. Spotting Rafe sitting all alone at one of the tables along the perimeter of the floor only accentuated the memory. For a man whose arrogance she had experienced firsthand, he looked surprisingly lonely. For a brief second, sympathy almost drove her over to talk to him.

"I'm not going anywhere near him," she muttered, even as she began to drift in his direction. When she realized where she was going, she added wryly, "I obviously have the willpower of a nymphomaniac."

"Who's a nymphomaniac?" Lauren demanded, startling Gina.

"Nobody, I hope," Gina retorted glumly, stopping in her tracks. She wasn't entirely sure whether she was relieved by the distraction, which was yet another fact that was worrisome. Was it moths that couldn't resist a flame and wound up dead because of it?

Lauren followed the direction of her gaze, then grinned. "Ah, yes, I heard about the kiss."

"Heard about it?" Gina asked, horrified. "How? From whom?"

"Half the town was at the rodeo. Word gets around. My source says it was more entertaining than anything that went on inside the arena."

Gina groaned. "Why did I do it? Why did I let him kiss me? And right out in public, yet! Wouldn't you think I'd learned my lesson about getting mixed up with smooth talkers after what happened a few years ago in Rome?"

"Could you have stopped him?"

"Not at first," she admitted. "He caught me by surprise, but later…"

Lauren's eyes sparkled with growing amusement. "Later? Then it did go on and on, just the way I heard?"

"Okay, yes, it went on a very long time. It was a very good kiss. In fact, it was a terrific kiss, which is why I am in more trouble than I ever thought it was possible to get into. I want to kiss a man who—" She cut herself off before she could finish the revealing thought.

"Who what?" Lauren asked, clearly fascinated by Gina's slip.

"Never mind," Gina said dismissively. "Have you seen Cassie? Did she come tonight?"

"She's here. She's busy hiding out from Cole. Seems to me she has her own problems with steering clear of intoxicating kisses," Lauren said. "And before you ask, Karen's on the dance floor, and Emma's out in the hallway on her cell phone. There's some kind of emergency back in Denver. Hopefully she's telling her boss or her client or whoever it is to take a hike. The woman is in serious need of a break. She's stretched so tight I'm afraid she's going to snap.''

"Emma can take care of herself," Gina insisted. "She's always been totally levelheaded and sane compared to the rest of us."

"Take another look. I was out at the ranch with her and Caitlyn earlier. I think even that little girl senses that her mother's at the breaking point. Caitlyn's birthday is coming up, and she told me the only thing she wanted was for her mom to move here because in Denver she never, ever sees her. How pitiful is that?"

Gina glanced toward the door and spotted Emma striding toward them, her expression grim.

"What's wrong?" Gina asked, regarding her with concern.

"One of my major clients in Denver has a problem. He wants me back there tonight."

"Are you going?" Lauren asked.

"What choice do I have?"

"You could tell him that you're taking the first break you've had in years and that he can just wait until Monday," Lauren retorted heatedly. "Sweetie, if you don't start looking out for yourself, who will? Certainly not those partners who are raking in big bucks from all those billable hours you put in each month, and certainly not the clients who see nothing wrong in tracking you down when you're supposed to be on vacation. How did he get your cell phone number, anyway?"

"All my clients have my cell phone number," Emma said defensively.

Lauren removed the offending item from Emma's grasp. "Which is a really good reason for shutting it off and letting me hang on to it for the rest of the weekend.

If you'd like, I can call this client of yours back and tell him that you've consulted your schedule and you are tied up in a very important negotiation and can't see him until the middle of next week. If it's a real emergency, he can speak to one of the other partners."

Emma stared at her in amazement. "You sound so convincing."

Gina chuckled. "She *is* an actress, Emma."

Emma shook her head. "Of course, she is. I just can't quite think of Lauren as anything other than the girl who used to spend the night at my house talking about boys until dawn."

"I had to talk about them. I certainly never dated them," Lauren said.

"Because you scared them to death. You were the smartest person in our class," Gina said. "That was very daunting, even to the boys with a B average."

"A fat lot of good that's doing me these days," Lauren grumbled. "Most of the people I deal with now don't even realize I have a brain."

"Which must mean that they underestimate you," Emma guessed. "Surely you can use that to your advantage."

"Maybe you two can trade services," Gina suggested. "Lauren can fend off your pushy, inconsiderate clients, and Emma, you can negotiate Lauren's deals. Nobody ever mistakes you for a pushover."

"Not a bad idea," Lauren said thoughtfully. "But we still haven't resolved this current situation. Shall I make the call?"

Emma hesitated. "Let me think about it."

Gina thought of what Lauren had said earlier about Emma's little girl. "Emma, think about Caitlyn. She's having the time of her life with her cousins and her grandparents. Do you want to spoil that by running home early?''

Emma blinked at the reminder, proof that she too seldom considered her daughter's feelings when work was involved. Then she drew herself up. ''You're absolutely right. Lauren, make that call. Tell Mr. Henley that he can contact one of the senior partners if he doesn't want to wait for me to get back.''

Lauren beamed at her. ''Punch in that number,'' she said, relinquishing the cell phone temporarily to Emma.

As soon as the call had gone through, she stepped away from Emma and Gina, speaking quietly but firmly to the offensive Mr. Henley. After she'd hung up, she came back smiling.

''He'll wait. By the way, what was that big emergency, or can't you say?''

Emma grinned. ''I can't say, but I can assure you that it wasn't life or death. Nor were any of his millions at risk.'' She reached for her cell phone, but Lauren shook her head.

''I think I'll hang on to this, at least for the rest of the night,'' she told Emma.

''But Caitlyn—''

''If Caitlyn calls, I know where to find you. Otherwise, your new secretary can handle anything that comes up.''

Gina chuckled. ''You're enjoying this, aren't you, Lauren?''

''It's actually rather nice to do something so ordinary. Maybe I should chuck it all and become somebody's secretary. I have terrific organizational skills.''

Both Emma and Gina stared at her.

''Have you lost it?'' Gina asked.

''Okay, maybe not a secretary,'' Lauren said. ''Organizational skills aside, I'm a little too bossy to take orders well."

"An understatement if ever I heard one," Gina said.

Lauren sighed. "You know who I really envy? Karen. She has it all. A husband who adores her and a ranch."

"Where she works too hard," Gina pointed out.

"I guess nothing's perfect, is it?" Lauren said. She glanced behind Gina. "For example, you have this absolutely gorgeous man staring at you as if you were more tempting than a banana split, and for reasons you refuse to explain, you're avoiding the guy."

All three of them turned to stare at Rafe, who was sipping on his drink, his gaze fixed on Gina.

"He's not interested in me," she protested. "Not the way you mean, anyway."

"That kiss I heard about says otherwise," Lauren said. "In fact, that kiss speaks volumes."

Emma's eyes widened. "Kiss, what kiss? That man kissed you? Did you want him to?"

"No," Gina said. "Yes."

A slow grin replaced the indignation on Emma's face. "Not sure, are you?"

"Of course I'm sure. That kiss was totally inappropriate."

"We can sue him for sexual harassment," Emma suggested, looking a little too eager.

"Settle down," Gina advised. "Nobody is suing anybody, and you are not taking on any cases in the middle of a dance, not after Lauren worked so hard to make sure you had the night off."

"I suppose not," Emma said, clearly disappointed. "But let me know if you change your mind."

"Do you look at everything in life in terms of the legalities?" Lauren asked her.

"Pretty much," Emma acknowledged.

"That has to stop," Lauren said emphatically, then glanced at Gina. "And you and I have to see to it. Find this woman someone to dance with. Are there any eligible males in the room? Other than Gina's guy, of course."

"Rafe O'Donnell is not my guy," Gina reminded her. "I'd be glad to turn him over to Emma."

"Whatever." Lauren surveyed the gym carefully. Finally her expression brightened triumphantly. "There," she said. "He'll do very nicely." She snagged Emma's hand. "Come on. Do you know him?"

"No," Emma said, hanging back.

"Then I'll introduce you," Lauren said.

"Do you know him?" Emma asked.

"No, but that's a technicality. Don't be a spoilsport. It's one dance, not the rest of your life."

Emma cast a totally uncharacteristically helpless glance over her shoulder as Lauren dragged her away.

"I see your friend is matchmaking again," Rafe said, coming up beside Gina and startling her so badly she almost dropped her drink. "Think she'll have better luck with those two?"

"Don't do that," she said irritably.

"What?"

"Sneak up on me." She avoided his gaze, pretending that his nearness wasn't stirring up all sorts of wicked memories of the kiss they'd shared earlier. She deliberately watched the drama unfolding as Lauren introduced Emma to the stranger, then left them to their own devices. After an awkward moment the man must have asked her to dance, because Emma allowed him to lead her to the middle of the gym. Neither of them looked especially happy about being there, but Lauren stood by beaming her approval.

Apparently satisfied, Lauren came back to where Gina and Rafe were standing. Gina noticed she deliberately inserted herself protectively between them. Rafe noted her action with amusement.

"Still protecting your friend, I see," he said.

"Of course."

"Trust me, she can defend herself. Did you hear how she doused me with ice earlier today, then made me hike all the way back into town?"

Gina regarded him with indignation. "I did not! You decided to walk back. I tried to stop you."

Lauren looked from one to the other, lips twitching. "But the part about the ice was true? Did that happen before or after the kiss?"

Rafe didn't seem the least bit surprised or embarrassed by the fact that Lauren knew about that. "Before."

"Interesting. I would have thought after." She grinned. "You know, an attempt to cool you off, so to speak."

"It would have taken more than a cup of ice to do that," Rafe said.

Lauren waved her hand as if it held a fan. "Oh, my."

Gina scowled at both of them. "If you two are enjoying yourselves so much, why don't I just leave? There are a lot of people here I haven't spoken to yet."

Before she could take a step, Rafe grabbed her hand. "Not now. I was hoping for another dance lesson."

She frowned at him. "The band's not playing country-western tonight. It's playing oldies. Surely you can slow-dance. Lauren, you dance with him."

"Afraid not," Rafe insisted with a perfectly straight face. "No offense, Lauren, but Gina's a little more patient with my stumbling attempts. Dancing is one of those social graces I never had time to learn. Too much studying. It made me a very dull kid."

"Then I'm amazed so many women invite you to society balls," Lauren chimed in, drawing a startled look from both Gina and Rafe.

"How do you know that?" Gina demanded.

Lauren grinned. "The Internet is an amazing thing. You'd be surprised what you can find out. I only scanned a few editions of the New York papers, and guess whose name popped up over and over in the society columns?"

Rafe regarded her with admiration. "I underestimated you, after all, Lauren."

"Many people do," Gina said. "Lauren, I think maybe you and I need to have a little talk."

"Tomorrow will be soon enough. There's a handsome man who's eager to dance with you. My hunch is he knows his right foot from his left, despite what he says."

She winked at Rafe, then added for Gina's benefit, "Just keep your guard up, sweetie. From what I've read about him, you don't want to cross him."

Unfortunately, Gina was already well aware of that.

Chapter Four

Since the whole purpose of coming to Winding River had been to clear her head and decide what to do to save her restaurant, Gina awoke at what she considered to be the unholy hour of 7:00 a.m. on Sunday morning determined to get on with that assignment. The only way she was able to drag herself out of bed was by reminding herself that it was nine in the morning in New York.

With Rafe turning up almost everywhere she went, the only way she was going to have any time to herself was to sneak out of her own house and take a drive into the nearby Snowy Range, where distractions were few and far between. And she had to do it before he turned up to accompany her or trail along behind like some sort of watchdog.

A glance outside told her it was the perfect day for going for a drive and then maybe even a hike. The sky was a crystal-clear blue with floating puffs of white clouds. The temperature had dropped overnight and promised to stay lower throughout the day. And there were no reunion events until the picnic at midday.

But before she could make her escape, she bumped straight into her parents, lingering over Sunday breakfast in the kitchen. They regarded her with surprise, no doubt because they so rarely saw her before noon.

"What on earth are you doing up so early, darling?" her mother asked. "You had a late night. It was after midnight when I heard you come in. How was the dance?"

Gina thought of the time she'd spent in Rafe's arms. For a man who'd professed to have no skill on the dance floor at all, he'd been astonishingly adept at everything from the waltz to the twist. Apparently it was only the Texas two-step that eluded him, despite his pitiful claim that he'd had no time for dances as a younger man. When she'd called him on it, he'd simply shrugged and insisted he was only following her lead.

As if, she thought dryly. She doubted he'd ever let anyone get a head start on him, much less lead him anywhere. She sighed at that. It was something she needed to keep in mind.

"The dance was fine," she said.

"Meet anyone interesting?" her mother asked, her expression just a little too innocent.

"What have you heard?" Gina asked, regarding her with resignation.

Her father frowned. "Yes, Jane, what have you heard? I'd like to know, too."

"Oh, for goodness sakes, it's nothing shocking," her mother said with a hint of exasperation. "Rose Ellen just happened to mention that Gina was with an incredibly handsome man at the rodeo yesterday afternoon."

George Petrillo seemed no more convinced by that innocuous explanation than Gina was.

"And?" he prodded.

"The man kissed me," Gina blurted, hoping to save them all the embarrassment of a long, drawn-out debate. "It was nothing."

Her mother grinned. "That's not the way I heard it. Rose Ellen said it made her toes curl."

"Jane Petrillo, I hope you weren't discussing your daughter's lack of discretion with half the town," her father said, his expression dismayed. As the owner of the local insurance company, he tended to worry first about what his customers might think. Gina had done enough outrageous, risky things with the Calamity Janes in high school to turn his hair gray. He always swore he'd taken out extra accident and liability insurance on the family just because of her dangerous shenanigans.

"No, of course not," Jane said, giving him a soothing pat on the hand. "Just Rose Ellen. She brought it up. I must say I found it fascinating." She turned to Gina. "I had no idea you'd brought a fellow home for the reunion. Why haven't we met him?"

"I didn't bring him. He's not here for the reunion. And you haven't met him because I sincerely wish that *I'd* never met him," Gina said, reaching for the car keys, even though the drive no longer held much appeal. "I'm going out."

"Where?"

"I don't know, but I won't be long."

She walked out before they could pester her with more questions. As she paused on the back steps to take a deep, calming breath, she heard her mother ask, "What do you suppose is going on?"

"I have no idea," her father said grumpily. "But I'm

sure half the town will know about it before we do. That's
what comes from letting her go off and spend all that time
in Europe. She's come home with a lot of wild ideas.''

''Oh, she has not,'' her mother said, then added wistfully, ''I just hope there is something more to this.
Wouldn't it be nice to see her married? I can't wait till
we have a houseful of grandchildren to spoil.''

Gina's groan was almost as heartfelt as her father's.
The speculation about her and Rafe O'Donnell was getting entirely out of hand and he'd only been in town a
couple of days. Right now all he was doing was shadowing her—okay, and kissing her in public. Just wait till
people around here found out what he was really after.

Rafe drove by the Petrillo house about 7:45 a.m. There
was no sign of Gina, though from what he'd gathered, she
was not exactly a morning person. Still, he found the fact
that her mother's car was missing this early on a Sunday
vaguely worrisome. Had Gina taken off in it? Would her
mother conspire to help her daughter skip town? Leave
the country? Maybe that remark Gina had made the day
before about fleeing to Canada had been no joke.

Because he hated the way his imagination was running
wild, he concluded the best way to get to the truth would
be to knock on the door and ask to see her. For all he
knew, the entire family might be at church, though most
had services that began later.

When a woman he assumed to be Mrs. Petrillo answered the door, he understood where Gina got her
beauty. Her mother was probably in her late forties,
maybe even her early fifties, but she looked a decade
younger. There wasn't a single strand of gray in her thick,
dark hair. There was hardly a wrinkle on her heart-shaped
face. But while her daughter's eyes were dark, Mrs. Pe-

trillo's were a vibrant green, and they were studying him with undisguised curiosity.

"May I help you?" she asked, when Rafe remained speechless.

He gathered his composure. "Actually, I'm looking for your daughter, Mrs. Petrillo. Is she here?"

"Ah," she said, her expression brightening. "You must be the mysterious man everyone is talking about."

"I'm Rafe O'Donnell," he said, taken aback by the friendly welcome. Obviously, the people talking were those who'd witnessed the kiss, and not Gina herself. He doubted she had painted him in a favorable light.

"My husband and I are just having a second cup of coffee, Mr. O'Donnell. Will you join us? Gina left a little while ago, but she shouldn't be gone long."

Never one to turn down caffeine or the chance to pump someone for information about Gina, he smiled. "I'd love a cup."

In the cheerful, yellow kitchen with its warm oak cupboards and white trim, she introduced Rafe to her husband and invited him to make himself at home.

"Were your ears burning?" she asked. "We were talking about you not fifteen minutes ago."

"Is that so?" he asked warily. "What did Gina have to say?"

"Not much, which is why I'm so glad you dropped by. You're not local, are you? How do you know our daughter?"

Now there was a minefield, Rafe thought. "Actually, I'm from New York."

"So, you and Gina met there?" George Petrillo asked, regarding Rafe with suspicion.

"Not exactly."

The vague response clearly stirred more suspicion on

her father's part. "We don't get a lot of New Yorkers around here. How did you happen to choose Winding River for a vacation?"

"Actually I'm working."

George's gaze narrowed. "You're not some fool movie producer, are you? They come crawling around here all the time these days, paying outrageous amounts for property. If it keeps up, the next thing we know we won't be able to afford to live in our own hometown."

Rafe chuckled. "No. I haven't even been to a movie in the last two years, and I am definitely not buying any property."

"Then what do you do?" her father asked, just as Gina's mother stepped in.

"George, you're pestering the man. Let him drink his coffee in peace."

"I'm just trying to get acquainted with a man who's got half the town talking about the way he kissed my daughter," George grumbled.

So they *had* heard, Rafe thought. That explained the interrogation. "I apologize for that," he said with absolute sincerity. It had been one of the biggest mistakes of his life, though he could hardly deny enjoying it.

"There's no need to apologize to us," Jane assured him, shooting a warning look at her husband. "Is there, George?"

"Not unless Gina objected," he said, scowling at Rafe. "Did she?"

Just then the back door opened and Gina stepped inside. "You!" she said when she saw him. "I thought that was your rental car out front. What are you doing here?"

"Looking for you, of course."

"And grilling my parents while you're at it? What a

lowdown, sneaky trick," she accused. "Did you wait until you saw me leave before knocking on the door?"

"No, I did not. And actually, I've barely gotten a word in," he said, regarding her with amusement.

"That's true, dear," her mother verified. "Your father has been doing most of the talking. I'm surprised your friend hasn't told him to mind his own business."

Gina directed a frown at Rafe, then her father, then Rafe again. "I'd like to see you outside, please."

He grinned. "Sure thing. Mr. and Mrs. Petrillo, it's been a pleasure. Thanks for the coffee."

"I do hope you'll come back and visit with us," Jane said. "Perhaps you could come for dinner before you go back to New York."

"Sorry, Mom, he won't be around that long," Gina said. "Will you, Rafe?"

He gave her a penetrating look. "My schedule is actually pretty flexible. Last I heard I'll be in town for at least two weeks."

Her mother beamed. "Then I'm sure we'll be able to work something out. You must be staying at the hotel. I'll be in touch."

"I'll look forward to it," he said, then followed Gina outside. Since she couldn't seem to stop pacing up and down, he leaned against the porch railing and waited to see what she had to say.

Finally she stopped in front of him. "I do not want you here."

"So I gathered."

"My parents don't know anything about my business. They don't know anything about Bobby. Leave them alone."

"I was not pumping them for information. In fact, I thought I was doing a darned fine job of evading all of your father's questions about how we knew each other and what I do for a living.''

"You didn't tell them you were a lawyer?"

"No."

"You didn't tell them you'd followed me out here?"

"No."

"You never mentioned Bobby?"

"Nope."

That seemed to silence her. Rafe couldn't help himself. He reached out and cupped her chin, forcing her to meet his gaze. "I'm just after the truth, Gina. Nothing else. If you have nothing to hide, talk to me, tell me the truth."

"You wouldn't know the truth if it bit you in the butt."

"You have a very low opinion of my ability to judge character, don't you?"

"Can you blame me? You've come after me as if I'm some hardened criminal, when I'm as much of a victim as any of the people you say that Bobby swindled. The man has all but destroyed my business. He has turned my life upside down. And because of him, an annoyingly persistent attorney won't leave me alone."

Rafe grimaced at the characterization. He'd always considered persistence to be a virtue, but he could see her point. Moreover, he was forced to admit that he was beginning to believe in at least the possibility of her innocence, but he was a long way from having any evidence for or against her. She might not see that as much of a shift in his opinion, but in truth it was a major concession. He usually trusted his initial gut reaction in any given situation, and he rarely let go of preconceived notions this easily.

"You could go a long way toward making your case, if you would just sit down and get this deposition over with," he pointed out.

"Not without my attorney present."

"Of course not, but isn't your friend Emma an attorney?"

"Yes, but her practice is not in Wyoming, and besides, she's here this weekend because she's overworked and badly needs a break. I'm not going to get her involved in this," she said flatly. "Hell, I'm here because I need a break, but I haven't had five seconds to think with you trailing around after me. I started to take a drive, but I stopped for coffee instead. I glanced outside and spotted you heading in this direction. I had this horrible feeling this was exactly where you were going. Lo and behold, here you are, sneaking around behind my back to cross-examine my parents."

"I was not cross-examining your parents," he repeated patiently. "I stopped by looking for you. Your mother invited me in. Your father did most of the talking. That's it."

She gave him a plaintive look. "Couldn't you go away?" she asked in what had become a familiar, wistful refrain. "Go home? I'll be there in a couple of weeks and answer every single question you have."

"Much as I would like to get out of the wilds of Wyoming and back to civilization, I can't take a chance that you'll disappear. You're my best link to Rinaldi."

"I haven't heard from him. In fact, if he's smart, I will never hear from him, because if I ever get five minutes alone with him, I will wring his scrawny neck."

She said it with such heartfelt conviction that Rafe's faith in her shot up another notch. That still didn't mean he could go running back to New York the way she wanted. Unfortunately, he was here for the duration.

And gazing into her sad, vulnerable eyes was making that more and more difficult with every passing day.

"I'll tell you what," he said finally. "I'll make you a deal."

She regarded him with suspicion. "What sort of a deal?"

"What's on the reunion agenda for the day?"

"A picnic in the park."

"Is that the last event?"

"No, most of us will be here for the Fourth of July fireworks later in the week."

He regarded her solemnly. "Do you swear that you will not skip town on me?"

She sighed. "I'm not going anywhere. How many times do I have to tell you that? You can turn your back on me. In fact, it might be nice if you just forgot all about me."

Rafe grinned at her wistful tone. "I can't do that, but I will back off. I have some paperwork to do."

"Hallelujah!" she said, though her tone was less than enthusiastic.

"I'm not saying I won't cruise by the park—"

"I should have known it was too good to be true," she murmured.

"That could be just because I'm longing for a glimpse of you," Rafe suggested.

"Oh, of course," she said sarcastically. "Why didn't I think of that?"

He was surprised by her skepticism. "You don't think that could be true?"

"You are not hanging around here because you're attracted to me. You're here because you want to nail me with a crime."

"Maybe that's how it started," Rafe said quietly, regretting the admission almost before the words were out of his mouth.

She gave him a startled look. "What are you saying?"

"I've already said it. Never mind. The point is I will try to give you a little space. Just don't make me regret it. I have a lot of resources and I will use them to find you, so save yourself the trouble."

He'd taken half a dozen steps, almost made it to safety, when she called out to him. He turned back.

"What?" he asked, noting the confusion in her eyes.

"Are you saying that kiss yesterday..." Her gaze locked on his. "Did it mean something?"

Rafe couldn't help the smile tugging at his lips. Her words were too close to an invitation, way too close to a dare, or maybe he'd just been searching a little too desperately for any excuse at all to do it again.

"I don't know," he said nonchalantly. He walked slowly back to her. "Only one way to find out."

Alarm flared in her eyes just as he bent down and lightly touched his mouth to hers. He could have stopped with that. He should have. But her soft little moan, the way she swayed toward him, they were too much. The next thing he knew she was in his arms and he was devouring her mouth.

The morning had been unseasonably cool up until then, but now the temperature shot up until it felt hotter than it had under the blazing sun on his walk back into town the day before. His heart pounded and his body turned hard, even as hers went pliant, molding to his in a way that left him shaken and her trembling.

His breathing was ragged when he finally pulled away. "I guess we have our answer," he murmured, his voice husky.

She stared back at him with dazed eyes. "Answer?"

"That kiss definitely meant something."

"What did it mean?"

He took a step back before he replied. "Trouble," he said quietly. "It was definitely trouble."

Trouble? Gina echoed to herself after Rafe had wisely walked away. It wasn't just trouble. It was a disaster. If he'd asked, she would have followed him straight to the nearest bed without giving it a second thought. She would have slept with a man who wanted to put her in jail.

Okay, maybe he was beginning to cut her a little slack, but he definitely didn't trust her, not the way a man ought to trust a woman he was making love to. Of course, that kiss had been all about lust, not love. Gina supposed a man—or a woman—could have spectacular sex with somebody without worrying too much about such niceties as trust. Personally, she'd never tried it. She'd had one serious relationship in Italy, but since coming back to the United States, she'd barely had time to date, much less get involved with a man deeply enough to think about letting him into her bed. And her relationship with Carlo had taught her all about the dangers of dating a suspicious man. His lack of trust, his constant accusations that she was deceiving him had destroyed them.

Now, in just a few short days, Rafe had stirred her hormones to such a fever pitch that she was willing to toss aside everything she valued for a quick romp with yet another man who didn't believe in her.

"I saw what Rose Ellen meant," Gina's mother said quietly, slipping up beside Gina and putting an arm around her waist.

"You saw?"

"Oh, yes. So did your father."

"I'm surprised he didn't go for his shotgun."

"I think he might have, if you'd shown even the tiniest hint of displeasure."

Gina regarded her mother with a wry look. "Well, that certainly didn't happen, did it?"

Her mother chuckled. "No, which begs the question, what is your relationship with Rafe O'Donnell?"

"I wish I knew," Gina said plaintively. "It's…it's confusing."

"Do you want to talk about it?"

She shook her head. "Not yet, Mom, but I'll tell you everything when I get it sorted out. I promise."

"If you want your father to run him off, he will, you know."

Gina grinned. "I know, and believe me, the thought holds a certain appeal." She uttered a sigh of resignation. "But Rafe would just come back again."

"Your father was a persistent man, too," Jane said, looking nostalgic.

"Did you ever try to shake him?"

"For a while," she said, then grinned. "But my heart was never in it. Is your heart really in getting rid of Rafe once and for all?"

"Apparently not," Gina said. In fact, she was beginning to look forward to having him pop up when she least expected it. As for those devastating kisses, she was pretty sure she was becoming addicted.

Chapter Five

Rafe had expected to be back in New York by Monday. Unfortunately, Gina showed every sign of sticking to her guns and staying in Winding River for a full two weeks. He'd hoped that his pestering would eventually wear her down, but she was clearly stubborn. Maybe that trait was also the reason she hadn't given in to the inevitable and shuttered Café Tuscany already.

He had been true to his word on Sunday. He'd steered clear of her, though he hadn't been able to resist taking a stroll through the park where the reunion attendees were gathered for their picnic. Gina had been playing baseball at the time, looking more carefree than she had since arriving in Wyoming. He regretted being the one responsible for putting a perpetual frown on her face, the worry lines between her eyes, but he had a job to do, whether he liked it or not.

Since it looked like he was stuck here, he had no choice

but to call his office and have his appointments shifted to other partners or postponed until his return.

Even as he dialed, he was dreading the third degree he was likely to get from his meddlesome secretary.

"Have you made contact yet?" Lydia asked in an undertone, as if he were on some sort of secret mission.

"Yes, I have 'made contact,'" Rafe said impatiently. "How are things on that end? Any word from the investigator on Rinaldi's whereabouts?"

"Nothing. Charlie Flynn says the man has vanished. He's probably basking in the sun on a beach in the Cayman Islands by now."

"Entirely possible," Rafe agreed. "What's the deal on the restaurant? Have you been by there?"

"It was operating at full capacity last night. I checked it myself. Gina's assistant has everything running smoothly. The veal piccata was as superb as ever."

"Did I pay for your dinner?"

"No, but now that you mention it, that's a very good idea. After all, it seems I was spying for you."

"If that's what you were doing, you must not be very good at it. You're not giving me anything I can use, Lydia."

"Because there's nothing to pass along. All I can say is that it's a shame that jerk's actions might bankrupt the place."

"Is the word out about Bobby skipping town?"

"It wasn't in any of the society columns, and Deidre, that's Gina's assistant, acted as if everything were perfectly normal. If there was any buzz about their problems, I certainly didn't hear it." She hesitated, then said, "You know, if you just stopped bugging her, I think Gina could keep the place open and pay back all the money Bobby stole. Not that she should have to, if you ask me, but I suppose somebody is obligated to make good on the investors' losses. Why not at least give her a chance?''

"If she's guilty of conspiring with her partner—''

"She's not,'' Lydia retorted, cutting him off. "I wish you'd just use that supposedly stellar gut instinct of yours where she's concerned. Have you spent a single minute with her? If you had, you'd know she's no thief.''

Maybe not, Rafe thought, but he refused to give his know-it-all secretary the satisfaction of admitting that just yet. Then there was the very intriguing question of how Gina was keeping the place afloat on her own. Assuming she wasn't involved in the scam—which he still considered to be a sizable leap—she had to be hurting financially.

Then again, Lauren Winters probably had very deep pockets. Even though Gina had insisted she wasn't going to burden her friends with her problems, maybe she had lied. Maybe Lauren was quietly bailing her friend out of her financial difficulties. Rafe wondered if he owed the actress a warning about what a risky venture she'd be getting into. Unfortunately, based on past experience, he had a hunch she wouldn't take the news well and that she'd manage to turn him into the bad guy.

"Lydia, cancel my appointments for the next two weeks. If that changes, I'll let you know.''

"You're staying?'' she asked, sounding more pleased than shocked. "Why?''

"Because Gina is staying.''

"How are you and Gina getting along?''

"Let's just say nobody's likely to nominate us for couple of the year.'' He tried to keep the regret out of his voice when he said it.

Apparently he'd succeeded, because Lydia sighed

heavily. "Then you're an even bigger fool than I thought you were," she said. "Romantically speaking, of course."

"Of course," he said wryly. "Sorry to disappoint you."

"You've been doing it for seven years. I should be used to it," she said with weary resignation. "But I keep holding out hope that one of these days you'll come to your senses, find a woman who can put up with you and settle down."

She paused, then added, "Now would be a good time, Rafe. You're not getting any younger, and you could do a whole lot worse than Gina Petrillo."

"So you've mentioned—more than once, as a matter of fact."

"It bears repeating," she said. "Bye, boss."

"Goodbye, Lydia. Hopefully they'll appreciate your humor in the unemployment line."

"Your threats don't bother me."

"I know. I know. All those bodies," he said and hung up. If only he could find a few of the skeletons in *her* closet. A woman as cheeky as Lydia was bound to have dozens of them.

If he was going to stay in Winding River, Rafe couldn't keep wearing the same clothes, especially since the only dry cleaner in town seemed to have a quirky disregard for customer service. Whoever owned the business apparently opened when he felt like it. If he had regular hours, they weren't posted, and Rafe had yet to see the lights on in the business.

The only clothing store in town offered Western wear. Rafe resigned himself to a new wardrobe of jeans he'd rarely have the opportunity to wear once he got back to New York. His closet was filled with practical suits and three tuxedos for all of the charity events he was duty-bound to attend because his partners' wives served on the boards and the fund-raising committees.

He left the hotel, walked down Main Street and was about to go into the clothing store when he spotted Emma Rogers accompanied by a little girl, who looked as if she might be about six. Emma frowned when she saw him.

"Still here, Mr. O'Donnell?" Emma asked, her tone not especially friendly. "I thought you'd be long gone by now."

"I'm afraid my business is taking longer than I'd hoped."

Her gaze narrowed. "What exactly is your business?"

Before he could respond, Gina came darting out of the café across the street and pointedly got between them. Ignoring the two adults, she hunkered down to give the little girl a hug.

"Caitlyn Rogers, you are getting so big I hardly recognized you. How old are you now? Ten?"

The child giggled. "No, Aunt Gina, I'm only six."

"I can't believe it." She leaned closer. "I think Stella has your pancakes on the griddle. Do you want to run on over there so you can get them while they're hot?"

Caitlyn looked up at her mother. "Is it okay?"

Emma regarded Gina with amusement, then turned her attention to her daughter. "Go," she said. When the little girl would have darted straight across the street, Emma reached out and caught her. "Hey, what do we do before crossing the street, even here in Winding River?"

Caitlyn regarded her guiltily. "Look both ways," she said, then dutifully did just that.

"Okay then, *now* you can go."

All three of them watched the child's progress, then Gina beamed at Emma. "We should join her."

"In a minute," Emma said. "Rafe was just about to explain why he's still in town."

Gina gave him a sharp look. "Was he really?"

He grinned. "Emma was certainly hopeful that I might. In all honesty, I was heading for the store to buy some clothes."

"You don't look like a man who wears a lot of jeans," Emma said. "In fact, if I had to hazard a guess, I'd say you usually wear thousand-dollar suits. I recognize the type. I go up against them in court every day. In fact, again if I were guessing, I'd say you're either a lawyer or a stockbroker, Mr. O'Donnell. Which is it? Or are my instincts totally wrong?"

Rafe looked to Gina for some sense of what she expected him to do under the circumstances. She sighed.

"Oh, for heaven's sakes, he's a lawyer," she said with no attempt to hide her exasperation. "Now that we know you have razor-sharp instincts, Emma, can we please go get some breakfast? I'm starved."

"Not until we clear up one more thing," Emma said, her gaze locked with Rafe's. "Why are you hassling Gina?"

"Maybe I'm just a suitor who won't take no for an answer," he said, enjoying the flash of indignation in Gina's eyes. Apparently she liked that explanation even less than the truth.

Emma's gaze turned to Gina. "Is he?"

"He's the most annoying man I know," Gina said with heartfelt sincerity. "And that is all I intend to say on the subject." She latched on to Emma's arm. "Let's go."

This time her friend allowed herself to be led away, but not before pointedly meeting Rafe's gaze. "I'm keeping an eye on you," she warned.

Emma and half the rest of the people in Winding River,

Rafe thought with resignation. Would a thief inspire that kind of protectiveness and loyalty? He needed to ask more questions about Gina, but doing so would stir up a real hornet's nest. She might never forgive him for unfairly dragging her friends and family into this, and for reasons he didn't care to examine too closely, that bothered him way more than it should.

"So, I was telling Mommy that I think we should live here forever and ever," Caitlyn told Gina, her eyes shining. "Grandpa has already gotten me my own horse."

"Grandpa ought to know better," Emma grumbled under her breath, then smiled at her daughter. "Darling, we live in Denver. You'd miss all your friends if we moved here."

"No, I wouldn't," Caitlyn insisted. "I already have a lot of friends here." Her expression brightened. "And I have cousins here. I don't have any cousins in Denver."

"She's got you there," Gina said, grinning.

"Oh, stay out of it," Emma snapped. "I don't see you moving back to Winding River."

"You never know," Gina said. Of course, if Rafe was successful in his attempts to make her part of Bobby's scam, she might be in jail instead, but it was seeming more and more likely that she was going to have to leave New York once this mess was straightened out. Customers could be fickle. If Café Tuscany's reputation was tarnished, they would stay away in droves. Any chance she might have of paying off the old debts would vanish.

She sighed, then realized that Emma was staring at her with a shocked expression. "What?" she asked.

"You aren't seriously considering coming back here to live, are you?" Emma asked. "I thought you had your dream job in your dream city."

"I do, but things could change."

"Does this have something to do with Rafe?"

Gina nodded. "Let it alone, though, Emma. You have enough on your plate without me dumping my worries on you."

"Hey, we're friends. Friends can always share their troubles with each other."

"Then why don't you tell me why you're wound tighter than a string on Pete Sampras's tennis racket?"

"Too much work, too little time," Emma said succinctly.

"Mommy is never, ever home," Caitlyn said. "She works really, really hard."

Emma winced at the matter-of-fact assessment by her six-year-old. "It's going to get better, baby. I promise."

Gina studied her worriedly. "When? I know you're thinking about taking on a big case here with Sue Ellen. How much time will you have if you're commuting between here and Denver?"

"I'll manage," Emma said tightly.

"And Caitlyn?" Gina persisted gently. "Will she manage, too?"

"Look, I'm doing the best I can, Gina, okay?" Emma stood up. "I have to get over to the jail. Will you take Caitlyn back to my mom's?"

"Of course," Gina said at once. She winked at the little girl. "But only if she'll go to the toy store with me first. What do you think, Caitlyn? Want to help me pick out some toys?"

Caitlyn bounced up and down on the vinyl seat of the booth excitedly. "Who're you buying toys for, Aunt Gina? Do you have kids at home?"

"Nope." She grinned. "I guess if we find something really, really special, I'll have to give it to you."

Caitlyn's eyes widened. "Really?"

Emma shook her head, looking amused. "You're going to spoil her."

"That's what an honorary aunt is supposed to do, right, Caitlyn?"

"Uh-huh," the little girl said solemnly.

"Okay then, have fun, you two." Emma kissed Caitlyn on the forehead. "See you later, sweet pea."

"Bye, Mommy," Caitlyn replied distractedly. "Aunt Gina, I was thinking. There's this really, really neat Barbie I've been wanting. Do you think maybe the toy store has it?"

"If it doesn't, we'll go find ourselves a computer and look for it online."

Caitlyn bounded out of her seat. "I'm ready. Are you?"

Gina drank her last sip of coffee, then joined the eager child. Truthfully, she was almost as enthusiastic as Caitlyn. Henderson Toys had been one of her favorite places as a child. She would save up her allowance for a whole month, then go into the store with her mother and walk up and down the crowded aisles studying the dolls and the trains and the board games before making her selection.

Sometimes, between the cost of an item and indecision, it was several months before she made a purchase. One memorable year, she bought a miniature stove, in which she could actually bake cookies, albeit very tiny ones. Her excitement over that purchase should probably have been a clue about the direction her life was likely to take.

Back on the street, they ran into Rafe standing outside of Henderson's his gaze locked on an elaborate train display in the window. The expression on his face was surprisingly wistful for a man whose every boyhood whim had probably been fulfilled.

Caitlyn slipped up beside him, her gaze every bit as fascinated as his. "It's a really cool train, isn't it?"

Surprised, he glanced down at her, then grinned. "It sure is. Do you like trains?"

Caitlyn nodded. "But I like dolls better. Aunt Gina is going to buy me a Barbie if they have the one I want."

Rafe's gaze shifted until it met Gina's reflected in the window. "Is that so?"

"It's not an expensive toy," Gina said defensively.

He frowned at her. "Did I suggest it was?"

"No. Never mind. Come on, Caitlyn. Let's see if they have the doll you want."

The little girl gazed up at Rafe. "You can come, too, if you want," she said politely. "I'll bet they have lots more trains inside."

"Maybe I will take a look," Rafe said, ignoring the frown Gina directed at him.

Inside, Nell Henderson rushed out from behind the counter to give Gina a hug. "And this is your family," she enthused. "How lovely that you've brought them in."

"Actually, this is Emma's daughter, Caitlyn. You remember Emma, don't you?"

"Well, of course. The two of you were in here often enough, right along with Cassie, Lauren and Karen." She beamed at Rafe. "They were some of my best customers, at least until they discovered boys. Then I lost them to the cosmetics counter over at the drugstore."

"I can't imagine why," Rafe said. "They're all beautiful enough without makeup."

Nell chuckled. "Oh, honey, you have found yourself a jewel."

"Rafe and I are not married," Gina said irritably. "We're not involved. We're not anything."

That threw the older woman for little more than a heartbeat. "Well then, you should work on changing that. A gallant man is a rarity these days. You should hang on to him if you're lucky enough to find one."

"Something to keep in mind," Rafe said, regarding her with amusement.

Bored with the adult conversation, Caitlyn wandered over to the dolls. She was back in seconds, clutching a Barbie in a fancy ball gown.

"This is the one I've been wanting and wanting," she announced to Gina.

Gina hunkered down beside her. "She is beautiful," she agreed. "You're sure this is what you want?"

Caitlyn's head bobbed, then she cast a shy look at Rafe. "What do you think? Isn't she beautiful?"

But Rafe's gaze was locked on Gina, not the doll, when he murmured, "Yes, she certainly is."

Gina's cheeks burned. "I thought you wanted to look at the trains," she grumbled.

"I'll come with you," Caitlyn offered, tucking her hand into Rafe's. "I've been here before. I can show you where they are."

Gina watched the two of them disappear at the end of the aisle, then sighed. When she looked up, Nell Henderson was grinning.

"Can't say that I blame you for sighing over that one. If I were thirty years younger, I'd give you a run for your money."

"There is nothing between Rafe and me," Gina repeated very firmly.

Nell shook her head. "Then that's a real pity, especially since the man looks at you as if you were the most fascinating creature he's ever come across. I haven't seen a look like that since the night my Herbie, God rest his soul, swept me off my feet."

Gina recalled belatedly that Herb Henderson had died just over a year ago. "You must miss him," she said sympathetically.

"Every day of my life," Nell agreed. "But I have my memories. That's something you ought to think about. Grab as many memories as you can, Gina. They're what carry you through during the difficult times. Otherwise, all you'll have are regrets. You don't want the last two words you whisper on your deathbed to be *if only*."

Gina heard Caitlyn's giggle, then Rafe's lower rumble of laughter. They were sweet sounds. She was already regretting that she had no claim to Rafe or to any family of her own, for that matter. Lately, she'd had no time to think about any future outside of Café Tuscany. With the restaurant's fate so much in doubt, she was forced to face the fact that without it her life would be unbearably empty.

She gave Nell's hand a squeeze, then went after Caitlyn and Rafe. She found them both watching an intricate labyrinth of miniature train tracks as half a dozen tiny engines sped around them on what appeared certain to be a collision course. But of course it wasn't. At the last second Rafe touched the controls and switched the tracks, sending the various trains safely past each other.

"Do you collect trains?" Gina asked him.

He shook his head and shut down those on the display. "Never had one."

"Why not? It's obvious you want one."

"As a kid, there were better uses for our money. Now I don't have the time to fiddle with a hobby."

"You know what they say about all work and no play, don't you?"

He regarded her seriously. "That it gets the job done?"

She groaned. "No, that it makes for a very dull guy."

A dangerous glint appeared in his eyes. "You think I'm boring?"

She knew exactly how he intended to prove otherwise, and a part of her wanted him to demonstrate, but there was Caitlyn to consider, and Nell. "Not boring, just limited. Under other circumstances, I might be tempted to try to change that."

"Oh? How?"

"Let me think about it," she said. "Maybe one of these days I'll give you a list of my recommendations. Will you pay any attention to them?"

"I might," he said solemnly. "What would my reward be?"

"More fun," she said at once.

He grinned. "You'll have to provide more incentive than that."

"Such as?"

"Will I get the girl?"

Gina shuddered at the penetrating look in his eyes. "I suppose that depends."

"On?"

"How badly you want her."

"I'm beginning to wonder about that myself."

He said it in a way that made Gina's breath hitch in her throat. She was thankful Caitlyn chose that moment to reach for her hand and give it a tug.

"Aunt Gina, since you're buying me a toy, why don't you buy one for Mr. O'Donnell, too?"

"His toys are too expensive," Gina said.

"That's right," Rafe agreed, his gaze locked with hers. "In fact, something tells me they're priceless."

Chapter Six

There had been times in her life—even after enduring Carlo's possessiveness—when Gina had deeply regretted the lack of a man who'd be there when she woke up and when she went to bed at night, a man who cared more about spending time with her than about his career. Now it seemed she had one.

It wasn't nearly as much fun as she'd anticipated.

Rafe O'Donnell was everywhere she turned, his expression remote, his gaze cool. The nonstop surveillance wasn't exactly what she'd dreamed of. In fact, it was all too reminiscent of Carlo. The fact that Rafe was so blatant about it grated on her nerves. She hated that everyone in town knew he was there to keep an eye on her for some reason that neither of them had revealed.

Other than her one conversation with Tony, Gina had refused to discuss Rafe's presence with her friends or her family. Only Lauren knew part of it—that she had to give a deposition when she got back to New York and that she wasn't looking forward to it. Cassie, Karen and Emma were studying her almost as intently as Rafe was, but their motive was concern, his was distrust.

He'd been at it for nearly two weeks now, though he'd stayed true to his word and remained mostly in the background ever since that chance meeting at Henderson's Toy Store over a week earlier. For some perverse reason Gina found that even more annoying and nerve-racking than having to deal with him. She was constantly on edge, continually reminded of the times they'd kissed and just how much she wanted him to kiss her again. For a few minutes in his arms she'd been able to forget why he was here. In fact, she'd forgotten almost everything, including her name.

His unexpected admission that he, too, had been affected by those kisses, had thrown her. Not that it made any real difference. He might be attracted to her, but he wasn't happy about it. In fact, Rafe didn't strike her as the kind of man who would violate his own ethical standards on a regular basis. Kissing a suspect, no matter how unjustly accused, was bound to be a breach of those ethics. No wonder he was keeping his distance.

Right now, for example, he was sitting in the booth next to hers at the diner, sipping coffee and pretending to read the morning paper. She knew it was only pretense, because his gaze rarely shifted away from her long enough for more than a glimpse of the headlines. She sighed heavily.

"You might as well come over here and join me," she said finally. Maybe they could discuss this like two reasonable people and find a way to peacefully coexist, since it was evident that nothing was going to make him go away.

He stared at her, clearly surprised by the invitation. "You sure about that?"

"Lately I don't seem to be sure about much of anything, but you're getting on my nerves over there, so, what the heck?"

A grin came and went so quickly she thought she'd imagined it. It was probably a good thing he didn't smile too often. She had a hunch the effect could be devastating, even more devastating than the rare hint of vulnerability she'd seen on his face as he and Caitlyn had played with the toy trains. Wondering what that was about had kept her awake for several nights, despite repeated lectures to herself that Rafe's past was none of her concern.

Carrying the paper and his cup of coffee, Rafe slid into the booth opposite her. Gina tried to pretend he was someone who'd come into her restaurant for a good meal, someone deserving of friendly conversation. She'd certainly been forced to be polite to a lot of arrogant, exasperating people over the years. What was one more?

"Still enjoying your visit to Winding River?" she asked politely, as if he were just another tourist instead of a man with an agenda.

"It's been interesting," he said.

"Finding much to do?"

He regarded her with amusement. "You know the answer to that, since I've pretty much been doing whatever you're doing. Are *you* bored?"

"I'm never bored when I'm home, especially with so many of my friends around."

"If you're so fond of this place, why did you leave?"

"I wanted to be a chef, a really good one. Tony ran out of recipes." It was a simplistic answer, but true enough.

"So you left here and went to New York?"

"Not right away. I trained all over at a series of culinary institutes here and in Europe," she said.

"Must have been expensive."

She had a hunch his interest in the cost had less to do with curiosity than with his desire to build a case that she'd needed Café Tuscany money to pay off old debts. She leaned forward and met his gaze evenly.

"I was very good. I received several scholarships," she told him.

"Is that how you met Rinaldi, at one of those cooking schools?"

"Yes," she said. "But before we go too far along that particular path, let's agree here and now to save all those nasty deposition questions for New York."

"It might not leave us much to talk about," he said, that grin sneaking back.

"Consider it a challenge. You look like the kind of man who thrives on challenges."

"I do," he agreed. "Okay then, you pick a nice, neutral topic. What shall we talk about?"

"Let's talk about you," she suggested. "Why did you decide to become a lawyer?"

"To protect the little guy from swindlers and crooks," he said readily.

Gina laughed. "Didn't take long to get back to your low opinion of me, did it?"

"That's your interpretation," he said. "Guilty conscience?"

"Not me." She regarded him intently. "Tell me something. Why did you take this case? Usually your firm is involved in much more lucrative, high-profile cases. You don't actually work for the little guys. You work for corporate America. Yet here you are up to your neck in a case that involves peanuts. Even if you recover every missing dollar that Bobby allegedly stole, your cut won't amount to much by your firm's standards. And just think of all the billable hours you're missing while you hang around out here keeping me under surveillance.''

He shrugged. ''I was due for a vacation, anyway.''

''But you wouldn't have chosen to take it here, would you?''

''No,'' he admitted. ''Probably not.''

''So why did you take a case that was going to cost so much for such little reward?''

''It was personal,'' he said, his expression turning grim.

''Oh? In what way?''

''My mother was among those Rinaldi swindled out of their money.'' There was a dangerous glint in his eyes. ''I imagine you can see why I'd want him caught.''

Gina was taken aback by the admission. She hadn't thought about Rafe having a mother—or any other family, for that matter—let alone a mother who'd backed Café Tuscany. ''How much did she give Bobby?''

''I doubt she viewed it as a gift. She *invested* a hundred thousand.''

She stared at him, openmouthed with shock. ''What? Where did she get that kind of cash? Forgive me if I'm wrong, but I got the impression the other day that your family didn't have a lot of money. Or were you just trying to play on my sympathy at the toy store?''

''We didn't. Not when I was a kid. My dad worked two jobs to keep food on the table. It was a constant source of friction between him and my mother. She was used to having the finer things in life, but she made the mistake of falling for a guy working construction on one of my grandfather's skyscrapers. Needless to say, my grandparents disapproved. They cut her off without a dime.''

He regarded Gina with a bleak expression. "At first I don't think it really mattered to her. They were doing okay and they were wildly in love. Then I came along, and the finances got a little tighter. When my sister was born, every dollar was stretched to the limit. My grandfather saw to it that my dad was never hired on the best-paying jobs."

Gina was appalled. "What a mean-spirited thing to do."

"You won't get any argument from me about that. It was the worst kind of abuse of power. Eventually it took its toll on the marriage, probably just as my grandfather intended. The fights got louder and nastier. My mother found richer companions. Ultimately my father tired of being humiliated and divorced her. He's living somewhere in the Pacific Northwest. We're not in touch, though I did get a copy of the newspaper announcement when he remarried a few years ago."

"I'm sorry," Gina said quietly. "His leaving must have made things even more difficult."

"It could have, but my mother is a survivor. She remarried a little more quickly, within months of the divorce, this time to someone my grandparents approved of. The money began to flow again, so my sister has had an easier time of it, despite the fact that the marriage only lasted a year. There was a hefty settlement."

His expression turned wry. "Then came another marriage, another divorce, another settlement. Financially my mother has done well for herself, but she's never found the kind of love she had with my father. While she's looking for it, she gets mixed up with guys like Rinaldi."

Gina was surprised by the depth of compassion she felt for him. His motives in going after Bobby and her made a lot more sense now. It also explained why he was distrustful, not just of her, but of all women. "So this is your chance to get even with all the people who've taken advantage of her?"

"Something like that."

She met his gaze with an unflinching look. "I had nothing to do with any of this. Unless she's been a customer, I don't even know your mother."

"You wouldn't have to in order to benefit from Rinaldi's con," he pointed out. "But I imagine you do know her. In fact, I suspect she's been a frequent diner at Café Tuscany, usually on Rinaldi's arm."

Gina shook her head. "Bobby never brought his women to the restaurant. They would've distracted him from cooking. Whatever else can be said about Bobby—and at the moment, there's quite a lot I could say—he was a total professional in the kitchen. Nobody except employees was allowed back there, not even his investors. He gave them a private tour a few days before our official opening, but told them it was off-limits from that moment on."

There was no mistaking the disbelief in Rafe's expression. "Are you sure he wasn't inviting guests in for a little after-hours hanky-panky?"

"If you mean his women, no. We had an agreement."

Rafe grinned at that. "Yeah, he had one with my mother, too. It wasn't worth the paper it was written on."

"But—"

He held up his hand. "Don't even try to defend him, Gina. The man is a con artist."

"And you think I am, as well," she concluded.

"The jury's still out on that, but at the very least you demonstrated lousy judgment in choosing your business partner. Whose idea was it for the two of you to go into business together, anyway? Yours or Rinaldi's?"

"I'm not going to answer that," she said. "Frankly, you should know better than to ask."

"We're just chatting," he said blandly. "Getting acquainted."

"We're already acquainted. I think getting to know each other any better would be a risky business."

"You could be right about that," he agreed with apparent regret.

Before they could continue, several of Gina's friends showed up. Radiating indignation, they stood beside the table glaring at Rafe. They might not understand what was going on between Gina and him, but obviously they were prepared to leap to her defense.

"What is *he* doing here?" Emma demanded. "Is he harassing you again?"

"No. He was here all alone. Since I was killing time waiting for you guys, I took pity on him and invited him to join me," Gina admitted.

"Why?" Emma said. She gave Gina an apologetic look. "I bugged Lauren till she told me about the deposition. Sorry. He's not trying to question you without counsel present, is he?"

Rafe chuckled. "I wouldn't dream of it."

Emma drew herself up. "I should hope not. I'd have you disbarred."

Gina grinned. "As you know, Emma is an attorney."

"Yours?" Rafe asked. "Did you change your mind and hire her?"

"No," Gina said.

"But I will be if she needs me, and if she needs a New York attorney, I can arrange that, too," Emma responded, gaze narrowed. "Does she need legal representation?"

"Not if she's innocent."

"Innocent of what?" Emma asked.

"Never mind. I am," Gina said.

"Back up a minute," Lauren said. "I thought she was just some sort of witness you were trying to question. Why is there any doubt about Gina's innocence? Gina has never done anything illegal in her entire life."

"Not even when Cassie begged her to," Karen said in an obvious attempt to lighten the tense mood. "She was always the voice of calm and reason." She grinned. "Not that the rest of us ever paid any attention to her."

Gina held up a hand to prevent a recitation of the pranks the Calamity Janes had been involved with years ago. A few of them might have skirted the fringes of the law. A clever attorney—which Rafe most definitely was— might be able to use them to suggest a pattern of behavior likely to culminate in this massive swindle.

"Let's not go there," she pleaded. "Could we change the subject?"

"In a minute," Emma promised. "First, I'd like to re- mind Mr. O'Donnell that sometimes the innocent need better representation than the guilty, especially if some shark is out to get them." She regarded Rafe pointedly. "Watch your step, Mr. O'Donnell."

Her gaze shifted to Gina. "Stay away from him," she advised.

"I wish I could," Gina told her.

"I'm crushed," he said.

"Something tells me a freight train couldn't crush *your* ego," she retorted.

"Making judgments about me again?"

She shrugged. "I guess that makes us even, doesn't it?"

He laughed and slid from the booth. "See you around, Gina."

"I'm sure," she said with a heartfelt sigh.

Somehow, though, in the last few minutes she had discovered that Rafe was far more complex and intriguing than she'd originally guessed. That made the prospect of bumping into him everywhere she turned a lot less daunting. She figured that was a very bad sign, given that the man wanted to lock her away.

Rafe assumed Gina wouldn't be going anywhere for a while. He had a feeling these friendly gabfests went on and on once the five women got together. Just in case he was wrong, he walked down the block, leaned against the bumper of his rental car and placed a call on his cell phone to the paralegal who was doing follow-up on the case back in New York.

"Have you been able to get into the bank records of Café Tuscany or Rinaldi or Petrillo yet?" he asked Joan Lansing.

"The judge is looking over the paperwork now," Joan told him. "We should know something before the end of the day."

"I need those records. We need to see if any withdrawals and deposits match up."

"I know, boss. I think we made a good case to the judge, though, if you ask me, that money is in some offshore account by now, not in a personal checking account at the corner bank."

Rafe sighed. "You're probably right, but we need to know for certain."

"Anything else I can do on this end?"

"Stay on that investigator. He should have found something on Rinaldi's whereabouts by now."

"Will do. No clues from Ms. Petrillo?"

"None. I'm actually beginning to believe she might not

know anything, not about the con and not about Rinaldi's disappearance.''

"How is that possible? They were partners.''

"We already know the man was a smooth operator. She could have been taken in by him, too.''

"Uh-oh, boss. I think I hear that knight on a white horse charging to the rescue.''

"Could be,'' he conceded. "But please don't tell Lydia. She'll never let me hear the end of it.''

He glanced up just in time to see Gina and the other women emerging from Stella's. They piled into Lauren's fancy sports utility vehicle. Rafe got behind the wheel of his own rental car and started after them. His pulse began to pound when he realized they were heading straight for the small airstrip on the outskirts of town.

Sure enough, Lauren turned in, drove to a hangar operated by a charter company and parked. Blood boiling, Rafe stalked across the tarmac to intercept them.

"Going somewhere?'' he asked Gina.

"You followed us?'' she countered, her expression indignant.

"Of course I did. It's a good thing, too. Are you planning on skipping town?''

"Oh, for heaven's sakes,'' Emma snapped. "There is nothing to prevent her from going anywhere, Mr. O'Donnell. Back off.''

"I can't do that.''

"Then you'll have to charter your own plane, because you're not getting on board with us,'' Lauren snapped.

Rafe ignored them both and kept his gaze on Gina. "Why the sudden decision to run?''

"I'm not running anywhere.''

"Then why didn't you mention this trip when we were talking?''

"It didn't come up. Besides, Lauren was still working out the details. I didn't know if we were going."

"Going where?" he asked.

She frowned at him, but she answered with barely concealed impatience. "I am going to Denver with my friends because Cassie's mother is having surgery. We want to be there to support her. It's not a big deal. We'll be back in a day or so, as soon as we know that everything's okay."

Rafe caught the unmistakable worry in her eyes, the hint of urgency in her voice. Because of his career, because of his mother's short-term attention span with men, he was a cynical man. There weren't a lot of people he trusted. Something told him he could trust Gina, at least about this.

Finally he nodded and stepped out of her path. "Don't make me regret this," he warned.

"I won't," she promised. Her lips curved into the beginnings of a smile. "Careful, Rafe. Someone might get the idea that you have a heart."

"They'd be wrong," he said tightly, then watched her go. As she was about to take the final step into the plane, he called to her. She looked back. "I hope everything goes okay with Cassie's mother."

She acknowledged his words with a wave, then disappeared inside the plane. Rafe walked slowly back into the hangar, then crossed to the office.

Inside, he found a middle-aged woman chatting on the phone. She glanced up, murmured something to whoever was on the other end of the line, then smiled at Rafe.

"What can I do for you?"

"That charter you've got going out, did the pilot file a flight plan?"

"He sure did. Plus, when Lauren called, she told me where they're going."

"Which is?"

Her gaze narrowed. "Are you with the media?"

"No."

"Because I'm not doing or saying anything that's going to get that woman's picture splashed all over one of those supermarket tabloids. When she's around here, she's among friends. What she does and where she goes is nobody's business."

"Believe it or not, I don't give two hoots about where Lauren Winters goes, but I do care about her friend Gina. I need to know where that plane is headed."

Her eyes widened at his fierce tone. "Is Gina in some kind of trouble?"

"That depends on where that flight is going."

"Denver," she told him finally. "They're going to Denver to be there for Cassie while her mom has her surgery."

Relief flooded through Rafe. Gina hadn't lied to him. "Good," he murmured. "That's great."

The woman regarded him with a puzzled expression. "You think it's great that Cassie's mother is having surgery?"

"No, of course not." Any explanation he tried to give would be way too complicated and unnecessary. "Never mind. Thanks for the information."

"Sure thing."

Rafe felt lighter somehow as he drove back into town. For once in his life his trust hadn't been misplaced.

Of course, it remained to be seen if Gina actually showed up back in Winding River when this mission of mercy ended. Something told him that until she came back again, he was going to be doing a lot of pacing and worrying.

Chapter Seven

Rafe was not used to having time on his hands. He didn't like being idle. Worse, he realized that he actually missed Gina, and not just because he couldn't ask a few more sneaky questions in an attempt to learn something new about Rinaldi and the missing money. He also found it worrisome that her planned two-week trip was now creeping on into its third week with no sign of Gina in Winding River.

"Still in town?" a gruff voice inquired just before Gina's father slid into the booth opposite him at Stella's. "I thought you'd be long gone by now, especially with Gina out of town for the last few days."

"Unfortunately, I haven't finished my business here," Rafe said. "Can I buy you a cup of coffee?"

"Don't mind if you do," George Petrillo replied, signaling to Stella. "You never did say what your business here is, did you?"

"No."

George's gaze narrowed. "Is there some deep, dark secret to it?"

"No, it's just a confidential matter. I can't discuss it."

"Okay, then, let me think. What kind of professions take their secrets so seriously? You don't strike me as a psychiatrist. And given the way you were kissing my daughter, I doubt you're a priest. How am I doing so far?"

"Right on target," Rafe conceded, impressed with the man's deductive reasoning, if not the suspicion behind it.

"Then I'd say that leaves the law. Are you an attorney, Mr. O'Donnell? And if you are, what business could you possibly have that concerns my daughter?"

"I never said—"

"Let's get serious," George said, leaning forward. "Your being here is no accident. You're not a tourist. Your bumping into Gina way out here, when it just so happens that the two of you live in New York, is no coincidence. The way I figure it, you're either stalking her or she's in trouble. Which is it?"

Rafe admired the man's blunt assessment. He had a feeling that under other circumstances, they could get along very well. "I think you should discuss this with Gina, not me."

"The only person I'm going to be discussing anything with is the sheriff, if I don't get a straight answer in the next ten seconds."

Rafe nodded, accepting the fatherly concern and the determination he saw on George Petrillo's face. "Okay, then. I'll tell you as much as I can. I came out here because of your daughter. I'm handling a case involving her business partner. I thought Gina might have some information."

"Does she?"

"She says she doesn't."

"Then go home, Mr. O'Donnell. If Gina says she doesn't know anything, then she doesn't know anything."

"I wish I could do that, Mr. Petrillo, but I can't. Your daughter is my best link to Roberto Rinaldi. Sooner or later they're bound to be in contact."

"And when they are, I'm sure she'll let you know," her father said. "Gina's an honest, law-abiding citizen. That's the way we raised her."

"As reassuring as it is to hear you say that, it's not good enough."

George frowned. "You're not suggesting that my daughter is mixed up in whatever this Rinaldi fellow did, are you?" There was a sudden flash of alarm in his eyes. "Did he kill somebody? Gina's not in any danger, is she?"

"No, it's nothing like that, I assure you."

"Then what are you suggesting that my daughter's mixed up in?"

"I'm not suggesting anything. I'm just saying that I can't leave here until I know more than I know now."

George Petrillo sighed. "If this is all about some legal difficulty my daughter and her partner might or might not be in, what the hell was that kiss at the house all about? Was that just some sneaky tactic to try to get her to talk?"

Rafe felt his cheeks burn. He should have known better. Not only had his behavior been unprofessional, but both of those kisses they'd shared had been in plain view of Gina's neighbors or her family. The very least he could have done was to exercise more discretion.

"Actually, that was a mistake."

"Which time? At the rodeo or at the house?"

"Both times, to be perfectly honest."

"Then I suggest you keep your hands to yourself from

now on. I don't want to hear any more about any so-called mistakes. This isn't New York City, where two people can get away with anything. Around here there are reputations to be considered. Eventually you'll go on your way, but Gina has to live in this community.''

"I thought Gina lived in New York.''

"This is her home. New York is where she works,'' her father said, making the same distinction Gina herself had once made. "Keep that in mind.''

"I'll do my best,'' Rafe promised.

George bobbed his head, clearly satisfied that he'd put Rafe on notice. "See that you do,'' he said as he jammed his hat on his head and strolled away, pausing for a minute to share a joke with Stella before heading for the door.

After he'd gone, Rafe muttered a sharp expletive. Why was it that every time he was around Gina, her friends or her family, *they* wound up asking all the questions? He hadn't been on the defensive so much since he'd discovered in the middle of a trial that his client had been lying to him about almost everything except his name. And he didn't like the feeling any better now than he had then.

Nor was he crazy about the fact that he hadn't even discovered why Gina's trip had already lasted several days longer than originally anticipated. Just when the query had been on the tip of his tongue, George Petrillo had cleverly distracted him with his own barrage of questions.

The fragile trust Rafe had begun to feel for Gina was already wavering. He'd give her one more day. If she didn't turn up tomorrow, he was going after her. And heaven help her if she wasn't where she had told him she would be—at Mrs. Collins's bedside in Denver.

For some reason Gina wasn't the least bit surprised to find Rafe sitting in a parked car just down the street from her house when she finally got back home several days after she'd intended to. She hadn't been on such an emotional roller coaster in years. A confrontation with him fit right in.

She watched him strolling toward her, a sinking sensation in the pit of her stomach. *One word,* she thought. Let him say just one wrong word and she would belt him. After what she and her friends had been through, she was just itching to take her anger out on somebody.

Rafe bent down to peer in the car window. "You okay?"

"No."

He seemed taken aback by her response. "What's wrong?" he asked eventually.

"Everything."

"Are you planning on sitting in there all evening?"

She scowled at him. "I might."

Rafe shrugged and walked around to the other side of the car, then got in. He sat there, staring straight ahead, seemingly perfectly comfortable with the silence.

"Caleb died," she finally murmured, barely able to get the words out. "Karen's husband. He just collapsed and died. It happened while we were in Denver. By the time we got to the hospital in Laramie, he was dead. I've been staying with Karen at her ranch for the last few days." She glanced at him. "In case you were wondering where I'd run off to."

"Never crossed my mind," he said.

She almost managed a smile at that. "Liar."

"I'm sorry about Caleb," he said.

Gina regarded him with faint surprise. "You really mean that, don't you?"

"I do. I didn't meet him at the reunion, but I saw you

and the others with him. It was obvious how close you were. It must have been a terrible shock.''

''It was. I don't know how Karen's going to manage without him.'' Gina hoped she would never experience the kind of loss that Karen was going through. Karen was heartbroken and racked with guilt because she hadn't been there. Nothing anyone had said had been able to console her.

''She could lose their ranch,'' Gina whispered. ''That will kill her. It meant everything to Caleb, but I don't know if Karen can keep it running on her own. I would hate to lose Café Tuscany, but it's not the same. I love it, but it's just a business. Even I can see that. That ranch meant everything to Karen and Caleb. And there's this man, Grady Blackhawk, who's just waiting in the wings to take it from her.''

She shuddered at the thought. ''How can something like this happen?'' she asked bitterly. ''Caleb didn't deserve to die. Karen certainly doesn't deserve this.''

Gina glanced at Rafe to see how he was reacting to her tirade. Not until he reached over and brushed away the tears on her cheeks did she realize that she'd been crying.

''I'm sorry I'm so emotional,'' she apologized. ''I didn't mean to dump all of this on you. I just can't bear the way Karen looks, so lost and alone. She's one of my best friends. How can I even think about going back to New York in a few days and leaving her here to cope?''

''The others—'' Rafe began.

''Will be leaving, too,'' Gina said. ''Except for Cassie. She's staying because of her mom. At least that's the excuse. I think there's more to it. Her son's father is here and they have a whole lot of unfinished business between them. Lauren says she can stay a little longer. And Emma may be coming back and forth for a while.''

"See, Karen will have people to look after her."

"I need to be here," Gina said firmly. As much as she loved Café Tuscany and her life in New York, nothing was as important as this, as being here when her friend needed her. "I have to call Deidre. Maybe she can go on managing things a little longer."

Looking resigned, Rafe handed her his cell phone. "Call."

Gina accepted the phone, but before she could dial, she remembered the deposition. "Rafe, I'm not deliberately trying to avoid the deposition."

"I know," he said with something akin to admiration in his eyes. "You're a remarkable woman, Gina Petrillo."

Startled, she stared at him. "Remarkable? Me?"

He grinned. "Yes, you. With everything that's at stake for you back in New York, your first priority is your friend's well-being. That's an admirable quality. It makes me wonder how you ever got mixed up with a sleaze like Rinaldi."

"Just lucky, I guess," she said wryly.

"Make your call."

"I could…" She hesitated, then took a deep breath. "I could talk to Emma. Perhaps we could do the deposition here. I know you can't hang around out here forever."

"We'll worry about that later. Take care of your business. After that I want you to go inside, take a shower and then I'm taking you out to dinner."

"I don't know," she protested, though without much vehemence. "I'm beat. I'll be lousy company."

"You don't have to entertain me, Gina. But you do need to eat a decent meal and get some color back in your cheeks. How can I possibly go after you in a deposition, if you look as if you might faint at any second?"

"Oh, I think I can handle you any day of the week,"

she retorted, feeling better already at the prospect of a good battle of wits. She handed back the cell phone. "I'll call from inside. I don't need you listening in on my trade secrets. Give me twenty minutes."

Rafe grinned. "Should I call Tony's and make a reservation?"

"Winding River's not New York. Besides, Tony always has room for me."

Rafe regarded her with suspicion. "Not in the kitchen, I hope."

"No, I imagine he'll let us sit in the dining room just this once."

He nodded. "Twenty minutes, then. I'll be waiting in my car."

"You could come inside or sit on the porch," she offered.

"No, thanks. I think it's probably best if I give your father a wide berth."

"Really? Sounds as if there's a story there."

"I'll tell you during dinner."

Gina ran inside, gave her parents a quick report on Karen, then made the call to New York. Deidre was surprisingly reassuring.

"We've been packed as usual. The guys in the kitchen are managing. Ronnie's been amazing. You'd think he'd been running the kitchen all along," she said with evident pride. "You and Bobby trained them well. The food's as great as ever. If you need to stay out there, we'll be okay. You do whatever you need to do."

Gina thought of the stack of unpaid bills she'd left behind. "Deidre, there could be problems with some of our suppliers," she said reluctantly.

"I know," the other woman said. "I saw the bills. Don't worry. You left me with a stack of signed checks.

I've written a few to pay some of the suppliers who were starting to get testy, and I've spoken to the other vendors. We'll be okay, at least for a little while.''

Deidre hesitated, then added. ''Look, I don't know exactly what's going on, but I can tell there's a problem. If there's anything I can do, all you have to do is ask. You gave me this job when I really needed one—I owe you. I don't have any cash to lend you, but I've gotten real good at juggling creditors. I'll keep the hounds at bay for as long as I can.''

''Have I ever told you how terrific you are?'' Gina asked.

''At least once a day. Now let me get back to work. I've got a line of customers waiting to be seated.''

''Then by all means go. Thanks, Deidre. You're a godsend.''

Feeling vastly relieved by the news from New York, she took a quick shower, pulled on a pair of jeans, her boots and added a sleeveless gingham shirt.

''Where are you going?'' her father called as she passed the living room.

''Out to dinner.''

''All alone?'' her mother asked.

''No, Rafe's waiting.''

Her father's expression darkened. ''I thought I made myself clear to that man.''

Gina regarded him with alarm. ''Daddy, what did you say to Rafe?''

''Just that he needs to remember that this is a small town and I will not allow him to ruin your reputation.''

''How terribly gallant of you, but the warning is unnecessary. Rafe and I are just…'' She couldn't seem to think of a suitable word.

Friends certainly didn't describe it. And they were

more than acquaintances. Given the sizzle in the air each time they met, *prospective lovers* seemed apt, but she could hardly admit that to her father. Or even to herself, under the circumstances. She was pretty sure it was unwise, at the very least, to contemplate getting into bed with a man who was about to grill her. Surely she had learned that lesson after a few months with the suspicious Carlo.

Eventually she just sighed. "You don't need to worry, that's all."

"I'll be the judge of that," her father grumbled. "Be home by midnight."

"George," her mother protested. "Gina's a grown woman."

"Maybe so, but there's not a lot to do after midnight in Winding River except get in trouble, if you catch my drift. Why do you think we have all those shotgun weddings right after graduation every year?"

Gina planted a kiss on his cheek. "I'm a long way out of high school, but I promise that Rafe and I won't go down to the river and engage in any hanky-panky after dinner."

But, of course, now that the idea had been planted in her head, that was exactly what she most wanted to do. From the moment she had watched her best friend's husband being buried, she had desperately wanted to do something—*anything*—that would remind her that she was still very much alive.

Rafe promised himself he was going to be on his best behavior over dinner. No probing questions. No sneak attacks on Gina's credibility. And most important of all, no crossing the line—which meant no kisses, no lingering caresses, no steamy looks.

Obviously, he'd lied to himself. So far he'd managed to keep the questions, at least about Rinaldi, to a minimum, but he couldn't seem to keep his hands to himself. There were a million and one excuses for touching Gina. After all, he had to help her out of the car, didn't he? And it was only polite to slip his arm around her waist when they crossed the street, right? And that stray curl that skimmed her cheek needed to be tucked behind her ear, didn't it? Could he help it if his fingers brushed hers when he handed her the menu or lingered when her hand trembled ever so slightly? She'd had a rough few days. He was only offering comfort.

And pigs flew, he thought in self-disgust.

"Rafe, is there some problem?" Gina asked, studying him worriedly.

"Nope," he said flatly, then turned his gaze to the selections on the menu. He'd expected little more than pizza and spaghetti and was surprised to find far more intriguing offerings.

"Your friend Tony has quite a menu," he noted.

"He's added a few things since I worked here." She grinned. "I send him a new recipe for Christmas every year."

"Only once a year?"

"The locals can't accept too much change all at once. You'll notice that plain old spaghetti and meatballs is still on the menu. There would be a revolt if he took it off, but once in a while he can talk his customers into trying something new."

"What do you recommend?"

"The penne *arrabiata*," she said without hesitation. "The tomato sauce has a little kick to it. I gave that one to him when I was in here the other day."

Rafe chuckled. "Yes, I can see why something spicy

would appeal to you." He put the menu aside. "What about wine? Shall we order a bottle?"

"Only if you can settle for the house Chianti. I haven't been able to talk Tony into starting a decent wine cellar."

"Chianti it is, then."

As soon as the waitress had taken their order with a promise to let Tony know that it was for Gina and her friend, Rafe studied Gina. "You look better. How did the phone call go?"

"The restaurant is very busy. Deidre's holding the creditors at bay. I can stay on here a while longer."

"But not indefinitely," Rafe said. "Not if you expect to pull Café Tuscany out of this mess. You're going to have to go back and face it."

Her cheerful expression faltered. "I know, but just for tonight can we not talk about it?"

Rafe hesitated. "Look, I know I'm probably the last person you want to—or even should—discuss any of this with, but I'm a halfway-decent listener."

"I'm sure you are, but how do I know that you won't take every word I say and twist it? Let's face it, you're not out here because you want to get to know me. You're here because you think I'm guilty of a crime."

"Not guilty, just involved," Rafe corrected.

"What's the difference?"

"I *know* you're involved with Rinaldi, and I *know* that he's done some shady financial deals."

"That's guilt by association," Gina pointed out. "Because Bobby's guilty, then I must be, too. That's what you're saying."

Rafe shook his head. "No, I'm trying to keep an open mind where you're concerned."

She regarded him doubtfully.

"Okay, maybe when I first scheduled the deposition, I made some assumptions," he conceded.

"And now?"

"I'm beginning to think my secretary might have been right, though if you ever tell her that, I'll be forced to deny it."

"Your secretary?"

"Lydia Allen. She's a big fan of yours and your restaurant. From the beginning she told me I was crazy for suspecting you of anything."

Gina's eyes brightened. "I know Lydia. I should have realized who she was when I first spoke to her about changing the deposition. She's a regular at the restaurant. And she works for you? How fascinating. You must have some redeeming qualities, then, if you can keep a woman like that on your payroll."

Rafe winced. "She might not agree. In fact, she says she stays with me precisely because I need someone to keep me honest."

"You're scared of her, aren't you?" she said, clearly enjoying the discovery. "What is she? Five-two, a hundred and five pounds? And you're scared of her. I love it."

"I am not scared of her," he insisted.

"Oh?"

He grinned. "Actually, I'm terrified. She can make my life a living hell. In fact, she takes great pride in it."

Gina chuckled. "I'll have to call Deidre and let her know that Lydia's next meal is on the house."

"Which won't do much to help your financial situation," Rafe pointed out. "Nor will it do a thing to get you into my good graces."

Her gaze narrowed. "What would it take for me to get in your good graces?"

"Some honest answers."

"I've never lied to you, Rafe."

"But you haven't told me the whole truth, either."

"I will when the time comes."

His spirits, which had been astonishingly light during their bantering exchange, sank. "And that will be?"

"When we do the deposition," she said flatly, and turned her gaze to Tony, who was crossing the restaurant, a beaming smile on his face for Gina, a cooler acknowledgment for Rafe.

Rafe couldn't help the trace of envy that filled him as he listened to the warm exchange between these two old friends. He wasn't used to feeling shut out, all but ignored, especially by a woman. Nor was he used to the distrust that Tony made no attempt to hide.

After the man had gone to check on their meal, Gina regarded him apologetically. "Sorry about that. Tony's very protective of me, and he knows about everything that happened with Bobby and that you're here to keep an eye on me. He's worried about what's going on with the two of us."

"You mean romantically?"

She had the audacity to laugh at that. "Hardly! No, he's convinced you have ulterior motives, that you're trying to wear me down so I'll incriminate myself. He mentioned it after meeting you the other day."

"And what did you tell him?"

"That you were a lawyer. That seemed to be explanation enough."

The stereotype rankled. "Your friend Emma is a lawyer. He doesn't distrust her, does he?"

"No, but Emma grew up here. That gives her an advantage."

A few minutes later Tony returned with steaming plates

filled with aromatic pasta. He served them, cast yet another suspicious look at Rafe, then returned to the kitchen.

"It's no fun, is it?" Gina asked.

"What?"

"Being regarded with distrust."

"No," Rafe agreed.

She smiled happily at that. "Good. Then you know how I feel every time I catch you watching me."

"Yes, I suppose I do," he agreed, then leaned across the table, his gaze locked with hers. "But just so you know, sometimes when I'm watching you, it's because I find you both fascinating and stunning, and I can't take my eyes off you."

She stared at him, openmouthed, as he sat back and lifted his glass in a silent toast, then grinned. "Gives you something to think about, doesn't it?"

"Rafe, I don't think we ought to go there, do you?" she said, clearly flustered.

"Probably not," he agreed readily.

Unfortunately, he was pretty sure it was too late to derail that particular train.

Chapter Eight

The ringing phone woke Rafe out of a sound sleep, rousing him from a dream in which he and Gina were entangled on a feather mattress, engaging in some very slow, incredibly provocative acts. Even before he picked up the receiver, he hated whoever was on the other end of the line.

"Rafe, why haven't I heard from you?" his mother demanded in a petulant tone.

"Good morning, Mother. How lovely to hear your voice," he muttered, knowing the sarcasm would go straight over her head. "What's the problem?"

"The problem is that you are not keeping me informed. Am I or am I not your client?"

"You're one of them," he agreed, glancing at the clock and groaning when he realized it was barely 6:00 a.m. He and Gina had stayed out late the night before, doing absolutely none of the things he'd wanted most to do, which was probably why his dreams had been particularly steamy.

"The most important one, I should think," she grumbled.

"Actually you're the only one who's not paying me," he pointed out. "I took on your case pro bono, if you recall."

"I still think I should be getting an update from time to time. Have you found Bobby? Will I be getting my money back?"

"I haven't found Bobby. As for your money, we'll know more about that once I find out where he's gone."

"Well, if you don't know anything, why on earth are you vacationing in Wyoming, of all places?"

Rafe gritted his teeth. "I am not on vacation. I'm following a lead."

"Don't you have investigators to do that?"

"Sure I do. They cost quite a bit. Shall I put their expenses on your bill?"

Adele O'Donnell Tinsley Warwick sucked in her breath. "There's no need to be snide, Rafe."

"I'm sorry," Rafe apologized automatically. "Since I have you on the line, let me ask you again if Bobby ever said anything at all about any place he particularly liked, some country or city he might be holed up in now? Is he the kind who'd hide all his ill-gotten gains in a Swiss bank account, or would he head for the Cayman Islands?"

"Neither. When he was with me, he seemed quite content to be in New York. From my point of view, none of this makes any sense. I thought he was happy. I thought we were happy. We were together for five years. Well, most of five years. There was that period when I thought I might be in love with Mitchell Davis, but he turned out to still have a wife tucked away upstate."

"Yes, I recall," Rafe said wearily. Obviously, his mother made a habit of deluding herself about the importance of a relationship. He sighed, then asked, "What do you know about Rinaldi's business partner?"

"Gina? He rarely mentioned her," she said dismissively. "I got the sense that she was contributing very little to the business, other than a certain flair she had with the customers and preparation of some of the dishes on the menu. Bobby was the money man and the brains behind the place. I always had the feeling she was holding him back, that her thinking was far too conservative."

"Perhaps she had good reason for being that way, since Rinaldi was so irresponsible where money was concerned," he suggested.

"Bobby was a genius," she said at once.

His mother's criticism of Gina and her admiring tone when she spoke of Rinaldi, even after everything the man had done to her, made Rafe cringe. "Mother, are you anxious for me to find Rinaldi so we can put him behind bars, or are you hoping to resume your affair with him?"

"How can you even ask me such a thing?" she asked indignantly.

"Because I honestly want to know the answer," he said. "I get this terrible feeling in the pit of my stomach that you want the man back, even after everything he's done."

"Don't be ridiculous. He cheated me out of thousands of dollars. I wouldn't take him back if he begged me to."

"Glad to hear it," Rafe said, though he wasn't entirely certain he believed her.

"Now, tell me again why you're in Wyoming. Bobby certainly wouldn't go there. He hated anything primitive."

"They do have hot and cold running water here, Mother."

"You know what I mean. He was a sophisticated man." She paused, then added thoughtfully, "But that little partner of his wasn't. Is that it? Is Gina in Wyoming? Is she hiding out there?"

"Gina is not 'hiding out,' and she's every bit as sophisticated as you or I," Rafe said impatiently, aware the moment the words left his mouth that his mother would seize on them.

"Oh, dear," she murmured. "She *is* there. You're not being taken in by her, are you?"

"No more than you were by Rinaldi," he said dryly.

"Rafe, darling, do be careful," she said with a rare display of motherly concern.

"Believe me, Mother, in my profession, there are very few people I trust. And after growing up with your unpredictable serial marriages, there are even fewer women I trust."

"Well, that's okay, then," she said, sounding pleased. Clearly she'd missed the barb directed at her role in his distrust. Rafe sighed at the realization that she was as self-absorbed as ever.

Only after he'd hung up did Rafe realize exactly how pitiful his words were and how very badly he wanted Gina Petrillo to be the person who broke the pattern.

"Gina, sweetie, the phone's for you," Gina's mother called cheerfully after a tap on the bedroom door.

Gina groaned and rolled over, burying her head under the pillow. She had tossed and turned all night long, trying to escape the dream in which she was running endlessly after a shadow. Bobby's, no doubt. Not even her subconscious would let her catch him, because apparently on some innate level she knew that killing him was a bad idea.

"Gina, are you awake?" her mother called.

"Yes," she finally admitted. "I'll be right there."

For one fleeting second she allowed herself to anticipate hearing Rafe's voice on the other end of the line. She was finding it increasingly difficult to keep her guard up around him. Nor was she having much luck with keeping her hormones in check. Dragging on her robe, she picked up her pace as she went into the hallway to grab the nearest phone.

"Hello, doll," Bobby greeted her as if they'd parted only days before and on the very best of terms.

"Roberto Rinaldi, where the hell are you?" she demanded, shaking with indignation. "Do you have any idea what sort of a mess you've left behind for me to clean up? I have an attorney shadowing my every move. I believe you know his mother."

"Not Rafe O'Donnell."

"Bingo."

"Sorry about that. Not to worry, though. I'll get everything straightened out."

"How? When?"

"Soon," he assured her. "Gotta run, doll. I just wanted you to know to hang in there."

"Bobby, don't you dare hang up on me. Bobby! Dammit, Bobby!" She realized she was shouting at a dial tone and all but slammed the receiver back into the cradle. "Forget the consequences. If I ever get my hands on him, I'm going to kill him."

She looked up and realized that her mother was studying her with a horrified expression.

"Into the kitchen," her mother said quietly, but in a

tone that had always meant business. "I think it's about time you told me what's going on."

Gina sighed and reluctantly trailed along behind her. She paused only long enough to pour herself a cup of coffee, then sat at the kitchen table. "Where's Dad?"

"He's gone to work, thank goodness. If he had heard you just now, it would have sent his blood pressure into the stratosphere. Whatever's going on, we'll keep it between us for now. I don't want your father upset. To tell you the truth, I'm not sure listening to you talk like that hasn't shaken me a little bit, too."

Her mother did look pale. Gina sought to reassure her. "It was just a figure of speech, Mother. I'm not going to kill anybody."

"It didn't sound that way to me. What has Bobby done? And does that have anything to do with what Rafe O'Donnell is doing here in Winding River?"

Gina slowly stirred two teaspoons of sugar into her coffee as she considered just how much to tell her mother. She finally settled on the whole truth. By the time she'd finished explaining all of the sordid details about Bobby's scam, her mother was practically quivering with outrage.

"What an awful man!" her mother declared. "And that was him on the phone? If I'd had any idea, I would have given him a piece of my mind."

Gina couldn't help it. She grinned. "As impressive and daunting as I've always found your lectures to be, Mom, I doubt they would have had any effect at all on Bobby. He's pretty much immune to criticism, and I doubt he has much of a conscience."

"That doesn't mean he shouldn't hear exactly what I think of him. Taking money from all of those people..." She shook her head. "It's a crime, that's what it is."

"Which is why Rafe is after him. And me, for that matter."

"Surely Rafe doesn't seriously think you could be involved," her mother said, her indignation stirring all over again. "You are nothing like Bobby."

"Thank you, but Rafe doesn't know me as well as you do. He says he has an open mind. At the very least he's hoping Bobby will contact me."

"Which he has. You have to tell Rafe," her mother said. "That will prove to him that you want this resolved as badly as he does."

"What am I supposed to tell him?" Gina asked. "That Bobby called but wouldn't say where he was?"

"That's the truth, isn't it?"

"Yes, but all it proves is that Bobby knows I'm in Wyoming and that we're in touch," Gina said, feeling despondent. She was not nearly as sure as her mother that Rafe wouldn't take the news of Bobby's call and somehow twist it to fit his own scenario, condemning her in the process.

"You have to tell Rafe," her mother repeated. "Keeping it a secret will only make you look guilty if he finds out about the call later." She gestured toward the phone. "Call him right now. That's my advice." She bent down and kissed Gina's forehead. "I have to get going or I'll be late. You have a good day. This will all work itself out, I promise. People like Bobby eventually get what's coming to them."

"I wish I shared your conviction about that," Gina said, giving her mother a half-hearted smile. "But I will think about what you've said."

If only her parents had caller ID, she thought, staring at the phone, but in this small, friendly community such high-tech equipment was viewed as both unnecessary and in many ways impolite. No one saw any need to know who was calling before picking up the phone. Heck, half the people in town, her folks included, didn't even own answering machines. People didn't have the same desire for being connected twenty-four hours a day, seven days a week that they did in New York. There was a lot to be said for that attitude, but right now Gina regretted it.

When the phone rang, Gina jumped, then scowled at the offending instrument before picking it up.

"Yes," she muttered curtly.

"You didn't by any chance wake up on the wrong side of the bed, did you?" Rafe inquired cheerfully.

"Something like that," she said.

"I know the feeling. My mother woke me out of a sound sleep, which would have been bad enough, but she also ruined a particularly fascinating dream."

"Oh, really?"

"Just so you know, you were the star attraction."

"You shouldn't say things like that," Gina chided, even though the news was fascinating. "I thought we had agreed that there would be no more crossing the line."

"Did we? My subconscious must have forgotten all about that. Now then, would I be risking my life if I suggested breakfast at Stella's in twenty minutes? That's not crossing the line, is it?"

Gina thought of Bobby's call and her mother's advice that she share that information with Rafe. "Actually, breakfast might be good. I'll see you there. Make it thirty minutes, though. I'm only half-awake, and I usually don't do mornings. It'll take me a while to jump-start my brain."

"I suppose saying that it's not your brain that interests me would be a really bad idea," Rafe teased.

Gina laughed, her mood improving considerably. "A really, really bad one," she agreed. "See you soon."

As it turned out, it took her closer to an hour to shower, dress and walk to Stella's. Admittedly, she was deliberately dragging her feet. Every time she thought of Bobby's call and his refusal to even admit where he was, she felt more and more despondent. By the time she got to Stella's, she was crankier than ever. Finding that Rafe had finished reading the paper and was drumming his fingers on the table immediately put her on the defensive.

"I thought maybe you'd stood me up," he said as she slid into the booth opposite him.

"I told you I'd be here, didn't I?" she snapped before she could stop herself.

His expression turned thoughtful. "There's that tone again. Did something happen this morning to get your day off to a rotten start?"

"You mean aside from your call?"

He winced but said gamely, "Yes, aside from that."

Gina waited until Stella had poured her a cup of coffee and taken their orders before answering with the truth. "I heard from Bobby," she admitted in a rush, before she could change her mind. She didn't feel one bit better once the words were out.

Rafe nodded slowly. "I see. And what did he have to say?"

"Not much. He wouldn't say where he was. He wouldn't answer any of my questions. He just said everything was going to work out."

"For whom?" Rafe asked. "I don't imagine he was talking about the people he bilked out of their money."

"No, I imagine not," Gina agreed ruefully. "Anyway, I thought you should know, even though it doesn't exactly give you any new information."

"Thank you," he said solemnly. "I know it wasn't easy for you to tell me about the call."

She studied his face intently. "You don't think I'm holding anything back, do you?"

"Are you?"

"No, that's the whole story. The call didn't last more than a minute."

His expression turned thoughtful. "I wonder why. Does he suspect your phone could be tapped?"

"I doubt it," Gina said. "Bobby never has been big on prolonged telephone calls. Ironically, in his own way I think he just wanted to reassure me."

"Were you reassured?" Rafe asked.

"Hardly. I was furious. I want more than a patronizing pat on the head," she said, her fury stirring all over again. "I want answers. I want every penny of that money returned. I want to put this mess behind me."

For the first time since he'd tried to put her life under a microscope, Rafe regarded her with what appeared to be genuine sympathy. "I'm sorry," he said quietly.

"Why are you sorry?"

"Because it must be hell having everything you've worked for put at risk through no fault of your own."

Startled, Gina merely stared. "You finally believe I wasn't involved?"

He nodded. "I do."

"Then go back to New York," she pleaded. "Concentrate on finding Bobby and getting to the bottom of this. Do it for your clients and, unofficially at least, do it for me. Not that I can afford to pay you. My cash, as you know, is somewhat limited these days."

Unfortunately, before the words were out of her mouth, he was shaking his head. "I can't work for you. It would be a conflict of interest. And I can't leave. You're still my best lead. If Bobby contacted you once, he'll do it again. Next time we'll be ready.''

"Ready how? You're not going to tap my parents' phone, are you?''

"No, but a caller ID could help. Do they have one?''

"No, and my father will hate it. He doesn't know what's going on. I told my mother this morning, but we agreed that he doesn't need to know. It will only upset him, and his blood pressure is already bad. I mean it, Rafe. I don't want him involved in any way.''

"Then we'll find another way,'' he said, his expression thoughtful. "Maybe we should both go back to New York.''

"No,'' she said flatly. "I told you yesterday, I won't leave while Karen's under so much pressure.''

"Then you make a suggestion.''

Gina considered an idea she'd been toying with ever since Caleb's funeral. "I need an excuse to keep hanging around,'' she said slowly. "Karen will hate it if she thinks I've put my life on hold because of her.''

"Okay. Any ideas?''

"I could go to work for Tony,'' she said with a surprising lack of enthusiasm. She knew it would feel as if she was only marking time, but it was the best she could do. "I'd tell everyone I'm just helping him out for a while. Maybe he'd even take that trip to Italy he's been promising Francesca.''

"That keeps you in town, but how does it help with pinning down Bobby's whereabouts?''

"We could put the caller ID on the restaurant phone. Tony would agree. He knows what's going on, and he'd want to help nail Bobby.''

Rafe shook his head. "That's only a partial solution. Right now Bobby's contact number for you is at your parents' house. He can just keep right on using that. Unless..." His gaze met hers.

Gina's pulse skipped a beat at the heated look in his eyes. "Unless what?"

"Unless you moved in with me at the hotel," he said slowly.

"Oh, no," she said at once, despite the decided leap of her pulse. "That is a really bad idea."

He grinned. "I don't know. I think it opens up some fascinating possibilities."

"You would."

"Are you saying that you're not even a tiny bit intrigued by what could happen if the two of us were sharing close quarters?"

"I'm saying that your clients would be horrified to discover that you were getting up close and personal with a suspect. Not five minutes ago you pointed out that it would be a conflict just to unofficially help me out."

"I could always tell them that I'm keeping you under surveillance."

Gina laughed at that. "Is that what you call it?"

"Okay, do you have a better idea?"

She considered the question. "I'll get my own place," she said eventually.

Rafe seemed completely taken aback. "Your own place? That sounds awfully permanent."

Gina shrugged. "Who knows? Given the situation in New York, coming back here might be the smartest thing—the only thing—I can do." Ever since her conversation with Bobby, she felt as though she'd lost the will to fight.

"You're conceding defeat on Café Tuscany?" Rafe asked, studying her with a shocked expression. "I don't buy it."

"I may not have any choice. Deidre's keeping things going for now, but we can't keep playing this shell game with the creditors forever. Maybe declaring bankruptcy is the way to go."

"Surely you don't believe that! I thought you cared about that restaurant."

"I do, but isn't that what you've wanted all along, to drive me out of business?" she asked, unable to keep a trace of bitterness out of her voice.

"No. I wanted answers. I wanted Rinaldi to pay."

"And me," she reminded him.

"Only if you were involved."

"Well, involved or not, it's my neck that's in the noose. Bobby's not here to take his share of the heat."

"Dammit, Gina, we're going to find him. You just have to help me out. Don't give up now." He studied her intently. "What's happened to you? I thought you were a fighter."

"I was," she agreed, then added sadly, "but so was Caleb. Look where that got him."

"You can't compare the two situations at all," Rafe insisted.

"Can't I? An uphill battle is an uphill battle, whether it's a ranch or a restaurant that's under siege."

Rafe slammed his fist on the table. "I won't let you do this. I won't let you just walk away."

Now that she'd actually gotten the word *bankruptcy* past her lips, it wasn't nearly as scary as she'd imagined. At least then all of this would be over. Rafe would go away. She could put her life back together again.

"You can't stop me," she told him flatly.

He stared at her with an obvious mix of frustration and concern. "Don't do this. Don't give up."

"I'm not giving up. I'm merely accepting the inevitable," she said, just as Emma walked in.

Rafe regarded Emma with relief. "Thank God. Maybe you can talk some sense into her. I'm not having any luck."

Emma frowned, looking from Rafe to Gina and back again. "What's this all about?"

Rafe tossed his napkin on the table and stood up, gesturing for Emma to take his place. "She'll explain," he said, then added with a shrug, "or not."

Gina stared after him, startled by the depth of his apparent disappointment in her.

"Okay, start talking," Emma ordered. "And this time I want to know everything. I can't help you if you hold out on me."

Gina shook her head. She couldn't go through this again this morning. She felt too raw, too vulnerable. Again she saw the disappointment in Rafe's eyes, and shuddered. It seemed she was letting everyone down, including a man who hadn't had that much faith in her to begin with. What did that say about her? She was letting other people control her life, and that had to stop. She needed to take charge again, and the first step was talking to Tony. She might not know yet what she could do—or even what she wanted to do—about Café Tuscany, but she did know that she needed to stay right here in Winding River until Karen's life was more settled.

"Not now," she told Emma. "There's something I need to do."

"And it can't wait ten minutes?"

"No, it can't," Gina said.

"If that man has upset you in some way, I'll make him regret it," Emma promised.

"No, actually, that man has made me see things clearly for the first time in weeks."

She might find Rafe O'Donnell annoying and pushy and arrogant, but he was right about one thing: she was a fighter. It was past time she started acting like one and seized control of her life again, even if no one else agreed with what she was about to do.

Chapter Nine

After leaving Gina, Rafe was more determined than ever to track down Bobby Rinaldi and make him pay for his crimes. It was no longer just about the money. Unjust or not, most of the investors, Rafe's mother included, could afford to take their losses. Now, though, his concern extended to Gina, who was clearly paying a far higher toll than mere dollars.

The bleak, defeated look on Gina's face the day before would haunt him forever. He blamed himself for that, and for somehow leading her to the conclusion that the only way out was to declare bankruptcy and come home to Wyoming. That was the last thing he'd intended when he'd started all this.

He muttered a harsh expletive and faced facts. That was *exactly* what he'd hoped for when he'd come charging out here on his white horse determined to save the day for his clients. But that was before he'd known anything at all about Gina Petrillo and the kind of warm, decent, caring woman she was. For once in his life, he should have paid attention to his secretary. Not that he'd ever admit that to Lydia. There were some things best left unsaid to a woman who tended to gloat.

Without pausing to consider what he was about to do, he headed straight for Tony's and pounded on the front door until Tony came out of the kitchen and opened it.

"There's no need to break the door down," the man chided.

"Sorry. I should have realized you'd be in the kitchen and come around back."

"Or waited until the restaurant was open," Tony suggested mildly, though he stepped aside to allow Rafe to enter.

"This couldn't wait," Rafe said.

Worry immediately creased Tony's forehead. "It's about our Gina?"

Rafe nodded. "Yes. And she doesn't know I'm here. It's better if it stays that way."

"I imagine she would not approve," Tony guessed. "So, why did you come? I am *her* friend, not yours."

"That's precisely why I came," Rafe said. "I think she's about to do something she's going to regret and only you can stop her."

"Then we must talk." Tony beckoned him toward the back. "However, you will have to explain while I work. I am making pasta and I cannot stop without ruining it."

In the kitchen Rafe drew in a deep breath, savoring the aromas of garlic and tomatoes, oregano and basil, flour and eggs. He also took in the aging but spotless appliances, the floor that looked as if it had just been mopped to a shine. If this was where Gina had learned the basics of the restaurant business, she had learned from a man who obviously took pride in his work. The room was both cozy and efficient.

"Sit," Tony said, gesturing toward a stool. "If you would like coffee, you will have to pour it yourself," he added, already working with the dough again, stretching it with nimble fingers, then putting it through a pasta machine to form perfect fettuccine noodles.

"No coffee, but thanks."

Tony glanced at him. "What is wrong with our Gina?"

"She said she had told you about her business difficulties," Rafe began cautiously, in case she hadn't been as totally forthright with Tony as he had been led to believe.

Anger brought bright patches of color to Tony's cheeks. Rafe couldn't translate the word he uttered, but it was evidently not complimentary toward Bobby.

"If he were here, I would toss him in a pot of boiling water myself," Tony said with a huff.

"Join the club," Rafe said.

Tony seemed taken aback by the ferocity of his response. "I was under the impression that you thought our Gina shared the blame."

"I was suspicious of her, yes," Rafe admitted.

"And now?"

"I'm all but convinced that she had nothing to do with anything that happened."

"But not totally convinced?" Tony asked, scowling at him. "Then you can go. I have nothing to say to you, and you have nothing to say that I wish to hear."

Rafe smiled. "But that's why you must listen, because you believe in Gina unconditionally, because you will want what is best for her."

"Of course," Tony said at once. "But how? What help can I give her? She would never take money from me, even if I had enough to fix the problem Bobby has created.''

Rafe thought of her display of pride and knew Tony was right. ''Not money, but I do think she is going to come to you for a job. In fact, I think she is going to tell you that she wants to move back here and work with you.''

''She came here yesterday and said precisely that.''

''What did you tell her?''

''That she would be welcome, but that she should think about it. Obviously, you think the decision is as impetuous as I do. You think she made the offer not because it is what she truly wants, but because she thinks it is her only option.''

Rafe admired the man's quick thinking, as well as his understanding of Gina. ''Yes, that is exactly what I think. She's giving up, Tony. I think a lot of things have been piling up the last few weeks, including the death of her friend's husband, and she's throwing in the towel, taking the easy way out. She's convinced herself that she has an obligation to stay here for her friend's sake. I admire that, and in the short term it makes sense. But a permanent move?'' He shook his head. ''I don't think so. I just thought you ought to know that, so you don't take what she says too seriously.''

Tony's hands stilled. ''You want me to turn her down, even if she comes back and says she is certain it is what she wants?''

''No, of course not. Just don't count on her staying forever. She loves that restaurant in New York. She'll regret it if she gives up on it. She just needs a breather until her fighting spirit comes back.''

Tony's gaze narrowed. ''Is this some ploy to get her back in New York where you can drag her into court?''

"Absolutely not," Rafe said, offended, even though on some level he could understand the man's suspicion. He had not come here with good intentions toward Gina. Only in recent days had that changed.

"Then what makes you think you know what is best for our Gina? Do you care for her?"

Rafe debated lying, but Tony's knowing eyes would see straight through him. "More than I have any right to, given my role in all of this," he finally admitted.

The back door opened just then and Gina stepped inside, a look of grim determination on her face. When she caught sight of Rafe, she frowned.

"What are you doing here?" she asked suspiciously.

"He is learning how to make pasta from a master," Tony said, giving Rafe a wink.

"I had no idea you were interested in the finer points of making your own noodles," Gina said, her gaze locked with Rafe's.

"It's a recent interest," he said easily.

"I see."

"What brings you by, *cara mia?*" Tony asked.

"Do I need a reason to visit?"

"Never, but you usually have one. It has not been long enough for you to have given careful thought to what we discussed yesterday."

Once again she regarded Rafe with suspicion, but then she turned to Tony. "I still want a job."

"You have a job," he replied. "In fact, it seems to me you have been away from it too long, all things considered."

Color bloomed in her cheeks and she whirled on Rafe. "What have you been telling him?"

Tony interceded. "I do not need anyone to tell me things where your best interests are concerned. This business of yours does not run itself. Mine certainly does not and yours is more demanding, yes? Especially now.''

''Are you saying you don't want me here?'' she asked, a hitch in her voice revealing just how close to tears she was. ''I thought you just wanted me to think it over. Are you saying now that you don't want me at all?''

''Never!'' Tony said. ''You have a place here always. I just don't want you to use my kitchen to hide out from your troubles. I want you to face them like the brave woman you are.''

Her gaze flew from Tony to Rafe and back again. ''Is that what the two of you think, that I'm running away, that I'm hiding out?''

''Aren't you?'' Rafe asked quietly. ''That call from Bobby yesterday morning was the final blow, wasn't it?''

''No, the final blow was finding you in here conspiring with a man I'd always thought was my friend,'' she retorted angrily, then ran for the door, slamming it behind her as she left.

Tony started after her, but Rafe stopped him. ''I'll go. It's me she's furious with.''

Tony nodded. ''The job is hers if she doesn't change her mind. You understand that, don't you?''

''Of course,'' he said, then went to try to undo some of the damage he'd caused, not this morning, but over the past few weeks.

Gina ran until she was out of breath and had a blister forming on her heel. She was cursing Rafe O'Donnell every step of the way, with a couple of healthy epithets reserved for Tony, as well.

She was limping and winded when Rafe caught up with her. She noticed that he was driving, not running, which meant he'd taken his own sweet time about pursuing her.

He'd probably hoped that a little time and exercise would help her to work off some steam. It hadn't. If anything, she was angrier and more hurt than ever.

"Want a lift?" he asked.

"No."

"Don't be stubborn. Get in the car."

"No," she repeated, though the thought of all that air-conditioned comfort was way too tempting. "Go away. I don't want to talk to you."

"If you don't get in, I'll just be forced to park and walk with you. Then two of us will be miserable and courting sunstroke."

He would do it, too. She could see the determination in the grim set of his jaw. "Okay, fine," she said, grudgingly walking around the car to get in.

Rafe gave her a quick sideways glance. "Going anyplace in particular?"

"Away from you."

His lips twitched. "Now that you know that's out of the question, any other destination you'd care to try?"

"Home," she said finally, then added hopefully, "alone."

He shook his head. "Not an option. You don't need to be alone, Gina. You need to talk this out with someone who knows all the facts, someone who's a good listener."

"Someone who wants to put me in jail?" she added wryly.

"Not you. Bobby Rinaldi," he corrected.

She sighed and let that pass. She wasn't convinced about that yet. Catching Rafe with Tony had shaken her. She had been counting on Tony to be the one person totally on her side, the one person who would give her a fresh start, no questions asked. His refusal to do so was Rafe's doing and she wasn't entirely sure of Rafe's motives. Until she was, she wasn't discussing anything about Café Tuscany with him.

That didn't mean she couldn't enjoy his company, at least for an afternoon. Whatever else he was, Rafe O'Donnell was definitely a sexy distraction, a far cry from most of the men she'd crossed paths with lately. He was certainly an improvement over Bobby.

"Pull over," she commanded.

He regarded her with a startled expression, but he actually did as she'd asked. Pleased, she grinned. "That was easier than I'd expected."

"Care to explain what we're doing on the side of the road?" he inquired lightly as an occasional car whizzed past.

"Here's the deal. If you promise that you will not say another word about the restaurant or about my decision to stay in Winding River, I will go to Laramie with you."

He didn't immediately seize the offer the way she'd anticipated. Instead, his expression grew thoughtful.

"Why Laramie?" he asked.

She ticked off the reasons. "Because it is not Winding River, because we can go to a movie there, because I heard about a restaurant I'd like to try."

"Aha," he said, grinning at her. "That's the real reason, isn't it? You can't help it. Even when you're on some kind of break, you can't resist checking out the competition."

Gina frowned. "It's not competitiveness. I just happen to like food."

"Oh, really? When was the last time you actually ate a meal. I've been with you on several occasions lately, and though you talk a lot about food, you barely touch anything that's put in front of you."

"I haven't been that hungry," she said defensively.

"Do you want to go to Laramie or not? Last chance. I can always drive myself."

"Okay. Okay. Just point me the right way," he said.

Gina gave him directions, then sat back, and for the first time since she'd talked to Bobby the day before, she began to relax as the miles flew by. Rafe flipped on the car radio and found a soothing oldies station that concentrated on ballads. By the time they reached the outskirts of Laramie, she was actually feeling pretty mellow.

"Lunch first?" he asked as he drove into downtown.

"Yes," she agreed, suddenly starved. The restaurant she'd heard about was actually a coffee house with an interesting menu of salads, some of which she thought she might be able to incorporate into the Café Tuscany luncheon selections. Even as the prospect crossed her mind, she realized the incongruity of it. One minute she was ready to shut the place down, the next she couldn't help planning for its future. Maybe she wasn't as committed to giving up as she'd made herself believe. Funny how both Tony and, more important, Rafe had seen that when she hadn't.

Gina studied the menu and found two or three different salads that sounded intriguing. She regarded Rafe hopefully. "Do you know what you want?"

"I was thinking about a burger," he said.

She regarded him with undisguised regret, which he immediately picked up on. "What's wrong with a burger?" he asked.

"Nothing, but would you mind getting a salad with it?"

"Why?"

"Because I want to sample three of these, and I'll feel like an idiot if I have to order all of them myself. Not that it would be the first time. I once ordered half a dozen appetizers at a restaurant in Paris because I knew I'd never get back there. The waiter brought them all without a single comment, but the next thing I knew the entire wait staff and the chef were standing at the door of the kitchen staring at me as if I'd sprouted two heads.''

"Did that bother you?"

"No, but it kept me from taking notes," she said sorrowfully. "I tried to write everything down after I left, but I couldn't remember every ingredient the way I could have if I'd done it on the spot. It took me months of experimenting to be able to nail down some of the subtler spices."

"So what you're telling me is that I am about to help you steal some chef's recipes," Rafe said.

"I'm not going to steal them," she protested even though he looked more amused than appalled by the notion. "I'll enhance them."

"An interesting distinction." He glanced up at the waitress, then gestured toward Gina. "Talk to her. She knows what we're both having."

After she'd placed their order, Gina regarded him with a grin. "I like a man who's not afraid to let a woman take charge."

"And I like a woman with confidence," he said. "It's nice to see yours coming back. It's also good to see you thinking about the future. I'm glad we came here."

"So am I," Gina said, her gaze locked with his.

"Are we having our first official date, Gina Petrillo?" he asked solemnly.

Her pulse fluttered at the suggestion. "I don't know, are we?"

"It certainly seems that way to me."

"Dating could be complicated," she said with real regret. "Maybe we shouldn't even think about it until... well, until everything is settled."

"You're probably right," he agreed. "But that's not what I want."

"Neither do I," she admitted in a whisper.

In fact, right this second with her heartbeat skittering crazily, she wanted very much to be on a first date with this man. She wanted to get to know what made him tick, wanted to feel his lips on hers again, wanted to feel his skin heat beneath her touch. It had been a very long time since she had wanted any of that, even longer since she had needed it the way she did right this minute. In fact, the way she was feeling was more appropriate to a fifth date, maybe even a tenth.

As if he sensed her turmoil, perhaps even shared it, he reached across the table and clasped her hand in his. There was strength and warmth in his touch. As the pad of his thumb grazed her palm, there was even more—a teasing hint of smoldering sensuality. Gina swallowed hard. Her gaze lifted, met his.

"Suddenly I'm not very hungry," she said, watching closely for his reaction to the unspoken implications of that.

"Neither am I," he said without hesitation, his gaze unwavering. "Do you want me to cancel the order?"

She shook her head, then chuckled at his obvious disappointment. It gave her courage. "Get it to go."

Ten minutes later they had three carry-out orders of salad and a warm loaf of sourdough bread. Even though she felt almost giddy, Gina managed to get to the car without bursting into laughter at the waitress's knowing expression.

"She knew," she said, collapsing in the front seat with the stack of take-out boxes. "She knew exactly what had happened, that we wanted each other more than food."

"She did not," Rafe insisted.

"Oh, yes, she did," Gina argued. "She actually gave me a thumbs-up signal as we left."

Rafe seemed vaguely startled. "Oh, really? Now what do you suppose she meant by that?"

"I hope you're teasing," Gina said.

He reached over and skimmed a finger along her cheek. "Why is that?"

"Because otherwise I am about to make a huge fool of myself," she said.

"Oh?"

"I am about to suggest that we take all this food to a hotel room," she said. When Rafe remained silent, she swallowed hard. "Well, have I made a fool of myself?"

"No," he said, his voice suddenly husky. Though he'd been about to start the car, he dropped his hand away from the key and faced her. "But I want you to think about this. Is it really what you want? You don't strike me as the kind of woman to engage in casual flings."

She laughed at that. "If only you knew."

"Meaning?"

"Meaning that I have never engaged in flings of any kind, casual or otherwise."

His eyes widened. "You're not...?"

"You can say the word," she teased. "And, no, I'm not a virgin, though my experience is almost as limited. It's just that it's been years since I've had the time or the inclination to get involved with anyone. I try my best to forget about the last time I did."

"Why now?" he asked. "Why me? As you pointed out earlier, this isn't exactly an uncomplicated situation."

"No," she agreed.

"Is that part of the attraction? Because it's a little dangerous?"

She considered the question, then shook her head. "No. If anything, that would make me run the other way."

He regarded her ruefully. "I notice you're not exactly gushing with a hundred reasons why you've chosen me to break your self-imposed celibacy."

"Is that what you want? Do you want me to stroke your ego?"

"No, if there's any stroking to be done, I can think of other parts I'd prefer to have you touching."

Heat gathered low in her belly as his words sank in. "Then what is this hesitation about?" she asked.

He took her hand in his, turned it over and kissed her palm. "As much as I would like to take you to a hotel room and spend the rest of the afternoon letting you seduce me, I'm not going to do it," he said with obvious regret.

Embarrassment flooded through her. When she would have jerked her hand away, he held it more tightly.

"One of these days you and I are going to end up in bed together," he assured her emphatically. "Make no mistake about that. But when we do, it will be for the right reasons. It won't be because you're looking for a temporary escape from your problems."

"That's a lousy thing to say," she told him heatedly, but then the truth hit her. That was exactly what she'd been looking for. She'd wanted a distraction, something to make her feel alive, and a quick romp with an extraordinarily virile man would have accomplished that.

She forced herself to meet his gaze. There was nothing condemning in his expression. If anything, he looked as if he completely understood her actions.

"I'm sorry," she said in a voice barely above a whisper.

"Don't be. Having a beautiful woman find me desirable, whatever the reason, is never a bad thing. I'm just holding out until it's perfect.''

''That day might never come,'' she said.

''It will,'' he replied with total confidence. ''Sooner than you think.'' He gestured toward the boxes she was clutching with a white-knuckled grip. ''Let's go find some idyllic spot and have a picnic.''

''You're not afraid to be alone with me?'' she teased.

''No way,'' he assured her.

''I could get carried away.''

He laughed at the suggestion. ''Now, *that* is something to look forward to.''

Chapter Ten

Gina could have suffered from terminal embarrassment for throwing herself at Rafe, but he refused to allow it. By the time they'd shared their picnic, he had her laughing unselfconsciously again. Because of that, her feelings—and her respect—for him deepened a little more. So did the attraction, even though she couldn't seem to shut out the fact that their relationship had begun with his insulting belief that she could be a thief.

But as the days wore on with no more calls from Bobby and little for her to do in Winding River, Gina began to feel more restless than ever. She couldn't go on this way, not with Rafe looking over her shoulder—albeit with less suspicion. Cooking dinner for her parents and baking for her friends wasn't nearly enough to satisfy her urge to be back in the kitchen cooking for a whole restaurant filled with satisfied customers.

After her outburst in his kitchen, accusing both Tony

and Rafe of conspiring, Tony forgave her and let her fill in from time to time, but it wasn't nearly enough. She was drifting and she didn't like it. She had to do something to shake things up, something to get her life back on track.

Maybe it was time to get some sound legal advice. No, she corrected, the truth was, it was way past time. She'd been putting it off, pretending to herself that Bobby would show up and prove that it was all some terrible misunderstanding, a mistake that could be easily rectified. She had been deluding herself that he would straighten everything out so that she wouldn't have to make any of the tough choices. Despite everything, despite all the evidence to the contrary, she hadn't wanted to believe that a man she'd considered a friend, as well as a business partner, had betrayed her.

Clearly, she admitted with a sigh, she had been wrong. Bobby's intentions weren't honorable. And Deidre's juggling act with the creditors couldn't go on indefinitely. Gina couldn't ask her to stand in the line of fire forever. This wasn't Deidre's problem to solve. It was hers.

She needed to make a decision, then get back to New York to handle the fallout herself, whether she chose to stay open and fight, as Tony and Rafe expected her to do, or to disappoint them both, sell or close the restaurant and pay off everyone she could.

Even though she hated involving her friends in what was happening, she knew that there wasn't a better lawyer—a better advocate—around than Emma. Fortunately, Emma was scheduled to drive up from Denver on Friday morning. Gina resolved to be waiting for her.

She knocked on the front door at the ranch at ten, knowing that Emma would have gotten an early start. Mrs. Clayton greeted her with a smile and a glass of lemonade, just as she had countless times when she and

Emma had been teenagers. There was something comforting about it. In many ways so little had changed in the past ten years. The bonds she had formed back then were still strong.

"Emma should be here soon. Are you sure you don't want to wait inside?" she asked when Gina moved to sit in one of the rockers. "It's a scorcher out there today."

"Thanks. I'll be fine on the porch, if you don't mind. I need to have a few words in private with Emma."

"Then I'll get Caitlyn out of your hair as soon as they get here," Mrs. Clayton promised, wiping her hands on her apron and taking a seat beside Gina. "Caitlyn's going to want to get out to the barn to see her pony, anyway."

Gina grinned. "I don't suppose that pony is a bribe from her grandfather to keep her coming up here."

"Of course it is," Mrs. Clayton said unrepentantly. "Now that Emma's divorced, her father and I would give anything to have the two of them here all the time. I know Emma is very successful in Denver, but she hasn't been truly happy there for a long time. She just refuses to admit it. And Caitlyn loves it here."

"No doubt about that," Gina agreed. "And I think a certain newspaper editor might be pleased to have them nearby, too."

The suggestion brought a wistful expression to Mrs. Clayton's face. "Ford seems to be a fine young man. Emma could do worse. Of course, every time they're together for five minutes, they seem to end up in an argument."

"I've noticed," Gina said with amusement. "Don't you think all of that explosive chemistry is a good thing?"

"I don't know," Mrs. Clayton said skeptically. "I haven't seen any evidence that they have a meeting of the minds about anything at all. If Ford said the grass was green, I think Emma would contradict him and point out every single brown patch in the lawn. I listen to the two of them and shake my head. Whatever happened to that agreeable girl we raised?''

"She grew up and became an outstanding lawyer with a passion for defending the little guy. Arguing is second nature to her. If she'd been on the debate team in high school, they would have been national champions, but back then she hated confrontation.''

"Well, that's certainly changed, hasn't it?'' Mrs. Clayton said. "And I'm proud of all she's accomplished, I really am. I just wish she'd give poor Ford a break every once in a while.''

Gina patted Mrs. Clayton's hand. "She will. I predict that watching them will give Winding River more entertainment than any other courtship to come along in years.''

"I don't know about that,'' Emma's mother said, grinning at her. "They'll have to work for that honor. I've heard some absolutely fascinating things about you and that young man who followed you here from back East.''

Gina blushed, even as she insisted that she and Rafe were just friends.

"Maybe so, but if Emma and Ford were half as friendly, I'd be a happy woman,'' Mrs. Clayton said, then glanced at the driveway. "There's my wayward daughter now.''

Practically before Emma pulled to a stop in front of the house, Caitlyn tumbled out of the car. "Grandma, Grandma, how's my pony? I gotta see him right now. I missed him soooo much. Do you think he missed me?''

Mrs. Clayton winked at Gina, then reached for Caitlyn's hand. "Of course I do. Let's go to the barn. I think your grandpa's down there with him right now. He probably already has the saddle on, so you can go for a ride.''

Caitlyn's smile spread. "Really? Hurry, Grandma."

Emma emerged from the car, shaking her head as the two of them went off toward the barn. "I swear that pony is all Caitlyn talked about all week. Now she's begging me to let her stay here when I go back to Denver.''

"Why don't you?" Gina asked. "In fact, why don't you just pack up and move here?"

Emma's gaze narrowed. "Okay, what has Mom been telling you? Did she put you up to this?"

"No. This is my own idea, I swear it," Gina insisted.

"Yeah, right." Emma sat in the rocker next to Gina's and sighed. "That breeze feels good." She gazed enviously at the glass of lemonade Gina was holding. "And that looks wonderful."

Gina grinned. "If I hand it over, will you give me some free legal advice?"

"Absolutely," Emma said, reaching eagerly for the glass. "Talk to me. What's going on?"

"This is confidential, right?"

"You're asking as a client, then, not as a friend?"

Gina nodded.

"I don't think a glass of lemonade would qualify as a retainer. Give me a buck. That'll make it nice and legal."

Gina pulled the dollar out of her pocket and gave it to her friend. Emma tucked it in her purse and grabbed a legal pad from her briefcase. "Tell me," she said when she was ready.

"I'm in trouble," Gina told Emma then. "I just don't know for sure how much."

"Start at the beginning and let's see if we can't get you out of trouble, then," Emma said briskly.

As Emma took copious notes, Gina outlined the mess

Bobby had created, the financial disaster he'd left behind. "Right now my manager is juggling creditors, but some of them are bound to start getting impatient. Should I sell out and pay them what I can? Declare bankruptcy?" She regarded Emma despondently. "I hate this. I just hate it. If it were my mess, I'd take responsibility for it, but it's not. I'm so furious with Bobby, I'd like to see him strung up by his toenails and left to die."

"An interesting form of justice," Emma said, clearly amused. "I don't think the legal system has a provision for it, though."

"Too bad."

"Okay, here are the options I do see," Emma said. "Depending on your partnership arrangement with Bobby, you might be able to distance yourself from the problem, but that could take some very tricky and time-consuming legal maneuvering."

Gina shook her head. "As much as I would like to and even if it were perfectly legal, I can't duck out on my responsibility to make things right if I can. A lot of our vendors are small businesses. I can't just abandon them. And our investors gave us their money in good faith. I thought Bobby was paying them back with interest, but apparently they haven't seen a dime."

"It's probably not as simple as filing for bankruptcy. Not with Bobby missing, but you could start the proceedings. It would buy some time to reorganize the business. Your investors and creditors would get their money on a timetable established by the court. It's complicated, but I think at the same time you could sue Bobby for restitution of everything he stole." Emma regarded her intently. "What are the odds he still has the money?"

"I have no idea. I don't know if he stole it so he could go off to live on some Caribbean island or if he took it to pay gambling debts or if he ran off with it just for kicks.''

"Well, that doesn't matter. We'll sue just in case there's anything left to get back. I have a friend, a classmate from law school, who's practicing in New York. Since I haven't passed the New York bar to be licensed there, he can handle things on that end. He'll file the papers when we're ready.''

Emma's professional, no-nonsense approach gave Gina the first spark of hope she'd felt in days. "You really think we can straighten this out and save Café Tuscany?''

"Absolutely, if that's what you really want." She studied Gina with a penetrating look. "Is it?''

"Of course," Gina said without hesitation. "Why would you even ask something like that?''

"Because you're still here. Even with all this needing your immediate attention, you didn't run straight back to New York after the reunion.''

"Because of Cassie's mom and then Caleb," Gina said, feeling oddly defensive.

"Is that all?''

"Yes.''

"The funeral was weeks ago," Emma pointed out. "Karen's getting back on her feet. Are you ready to go back to New York?''

When Gina started to respond, Emma held up her hand. "You don't have to answer me now. Think about it. Something is keeping you here. Could be it's nothing more than a delaying tactic, because you haven't wanted to face what's going on in New York. But that's not like you. It could be that you're feeling the same pull that Cassie felt, the same pull that Lauren mentions from time to time.''

"And you?" Gina asked. "Are you feeling it, too, Emma?"

"Maybe," she admitted. "Just a little. Being here is good for Caitlyn. I can't deny that. And Denver is a rat race for me, no question about it."

"Then you have been thinking about staying," Gina concluded.

"Not thinking about it, not consciously, anyway. But the possibility is just there. I can't ignore it forever," she said with a sigh, then shook her head. "But we're talking about you now. I just want you to be sure you understand why you've stayed here, rather than go back to New York to kick butt and settle all of this weeks ago. *That's* what I would have expected you to do."

"Are you saying I've been acting like a coward?"

"I'm not making any judgments. You have to figure out what you really want before you make a final decision about how you want me to handle this."

Gina nodded. "You're right. I'll think about it and I'll call you before you head back to Denver."

"Take your time. I'm actually thinking about sticking around all week."

"Oh, really? Does Ford Hamilton have anything to do with that?"

"Don't be ridiculous," Emma snapped impatiently. "It's for Caitlyn. And because this case of Sue Ellen's I'm working on is getting closer to trial. I have witnesses to depose and a ton of last-minute details to handle right here."

Gina grinned. "Whatever you say."

"That's the truth."

"Maybe you should do some thinking over the weekend, too," Gina teased. "Maybe I'm not the only one whose feelings are ambivalent these days."

Emma scowled at her. "Keep it up and I'll charge you my regular fee."

Gina shuddered. "Then I really would go bankrupt." She bent down and kissed Emma's cheek. "Thanks, sweetie. I'll call you."

Emma waved, then called out just as Gina was about to get in her car. "By the way, one piece of advice for right now—steer clear of Rafe. No matter what he says about being after Bobby, not you, you can't trust him. From now on he needs to go through me."

"I don't think that's going to work," Gina told her, thinking of the way her relationship with Rafe was progressing and just how badly she wanted it to wind up in bed.

"Why not?"

"Because we're just a little bit beyond needing an intermediary."

Emma's eyes widened. "Please tell me you're not sleeping with him."

"I'm not sleeping with him," Gina told her solemnly. "More's the pity. But I'm definitely hoping that will change."

"Are you nuts?" Emma demanded.

"Nope. For the first time in a long time, I'm finally going after something I want. I'm paying some attention to my personal life."

"Do you want Rafe more than you want Café Tuscany? Because that's what this could come down to," Emma warned.

Her vehemence took Gina by surprise, but it didn't scare her the way Emma had obviously intended it to. That was just one more thing she was going to have to think about over the weekend.

* * *

Rafe was hunkered down in his room going through a pile of papers that Lydia had faxed to him just that morning. It seemed he was destined to run his law practice from a Winding River hotel for the foreseeable future. He was so caught up in his work that the pounding on his door startled him. Finding Emma Rogers on his doorstep startled him even more.

"This is a surprise," he said.

"Yes, I imagine it is," she said, her expression as fierce as her tone. "I imagine you thought you could try all sorts of sneaky tactics to get what you wanted from Gina and no one would call you on it, but I'm here to tell you otherwise."

"I have no idea what you're talking about. Why don't you come in and explain it."

She stepped into the room, took note of the piles of paperwork. "Working on the Café Tuscany case, are you?"

Rafe sighed. "Gina told you."

"She told me everything. I'm now representing her."

"Good."

She blinked at that. "Good?" she said, sounding ever-so-slightly more hesitant.

"She needs a strong advocate. Obviously, I can't be that for her."

"I'm glad you understand a little bit about ethics. I was beginning to think you were totally clueless."

He regarded Emma curiously. "What exactly has Gina been telling you?"

"I'm not at liberty to discuss that."

"And I'm not asking for details about Café Tuscany's financial mess. I'm asking you what she's told you about the two of us."

Emma seemed to be weighing the ethics of saying anything about that, as well. "Enough that I suspect you're crossing the line," she said finally.

"Did she say anything about objecting?"

"That's beside the point. It's wrong. You have to know that. Go back to New York, Rafe. You'll be contacted by an attorney there. Gina will come in and answer all your questions, and we'll get this mess straightened out."

"I'm not convinced Gina has any answers to my questions," he said.

"Then what are you still doing here?" she demanded.

"Bobby Rinaldi has all the answers. He's been in touch with Gina once. I imagine he will be again. Why don't you convince her to let us tap her phone or, at the very least, hook up a caller ID?"

"I'll discuss it with her."

"I've already mentioned it. She refused."

Emma's expression turned thoughtful. "I imagine she doesn't want her parents involved."

"So she said, but the bottom line is, the longer she stays with them, the more likely they are going to get drawn into this. Bobby will call there again. If her mother answers, I imagine he'll get an earful. Gina says her mother's fit to be tied and ready to tell him just that. Her father, however, doesn't know a thing, and she wants it to stay that way."

"Maybe I can convince her to get her own place and her own phone, at least temporarily," Emma said slowly. "I know she wants to locate Bobby as badly as you do. If he thinks she's giving up on New York and settling here, he might even risk a visit. He owes her an explanation, if nothing else."

Rafe nodded. "That was my thinking."

"I'll talk to her," Emma promised.

Rafe glanced out the window. "Now would be a good

time. Here she comes." He stood up and opened the door. "Come on in and join the party." Once she was inside, he retreated to the chair beside the desk. He had a feeling anyplace else would put him right in the line of fire. The two women were scowling at each other.

"What are you doing here?" Gina demanded.

At the same moment Emma chided, "I thought I told you to stay away from Rafe."

Gina shrugged. "I told you that wasn't going to work."

Emma looked from Gina to Rafe and back, then sighed. "Okay, here's a suggestion," she said to Rafe. "I'll make a deal with you. If you promise her immunity from all prosecution on this, she can help you catch Bobby. And I want it in writing."

"Done," Rafe said.

Emma looked at Gina. "Okay with you?"

"We won't be on opposing sides anymore?" Gina asked, her gaze locked with Rafe's.

"No. We'll be partners," he said.

A smile broke slowly and spread across her face. "Done," she agreed at once.

"If you decide to stay in Winding River for the time being, I also think you should consider getting your own place, at least temporarily," Emma said. "Unless you want to put some kind of wiretap or caller ID on the phone at your parents' place."

"I don't want them dragged into this," Gina said. "I think moving into my own place makes a lot of sense. In fact, I'm pretty sure the room next to this one is available." She glanced toward the wall and grinned. "It even has a connecting door. How handy."

Rafe groaned. "Now, Gina, we've talked about this. Nothing's changed."

"Sure it has. We're partners now. Where you go, I go, right?"

Emma moaned. "I'm out of here. I'll leave you two to work out the details. Rafe, I'll expect that agreement by the end of the day." She gave Gina a stern look. "Until I have it, could the two of you try to keep your hands to yourselves?"

"Not a problem," Rafe insisted, shoving his hands in his pockets.

But as adamant as he was, he wasn't so sure about Gina. That gleam in her eyes suggested she was not above creating a little mischief just to test his resolve. In fact, right this second she was regarding him a little too cheerfully.

"This is an interesting turn of events, isn't it?" she commented after Emma had gone.

"I suppose that depends on your point of view," he responded cautiously.

"Well, from my point of view what could be better than getting all those nasty suspicions cleared up? Now we're free to do whatever we want to do."

"Oh, really? Exactly how do you see this partnership progressing?"

"Well, for starters, you could stop lurking back there in the corner and come over here."

"Why would I want to do that?"

"So we can properly seal this deal."

He chuckled at that. "I think Emma would recommend a signed document for that."

Gina shrugged. "Emma has her way of doing things. I have mine." Her grin turned wicked. "I think you'll like my way better."

Heat shot through him. "I'm sure I would, but it's still

a bad idea. Sex can really complicate a business relationship.''

Her expression turned thoughtful. ''Is that what we have now, a business relationship?''

''Exactly.''

''That's not entirely how I see it,'' she said, taking a few steps in his direction.

Rafe began to feel crowded. His resolve was starting to waver. ''Oh?'' he said, his voice husky.

''Want to know how I see it?''

He had a feeling he'd better know exactly what was going on in that complicated brain of hers. ''Sure.''

She slid onto his lap and wound her arms around his neck. ''The way I see it we've been given a fresh start. We're on the same side. We're partners. And for partners to work together successfully, they should know each other very, very well. You might even say, they should know each other—'' her gaze locked with his ''—intimately.''

Rafe's breath caught in his throat as her hands slipped to his chest. She began to work the buttons of his shirt free. Each time her knuckles skimmed across bare skin, a shock jolted through him. He caught her hands and held them still as he met her gaze.

''That agreement isn't drawn up and signed yet,'' he reminded her.

''That's okay. I trust you.''

''Do you? Emma would advise you against that.''

''What does she know?''

''Quite a lot, as it happens. You hired her, didn't you? She's looking out for your best interests. You should pay attention to her.''

''I'd rather pay attention to you right now.''

Before he could stop her, her wickedly clever mouth

settled on his. In no time at all she had his thinking mud-
dled and his breath hitching. When the kiss ended, his
resolve was in tatters, but he made one last valiant attempt
to make her see reason.

Gina merely smiled knowingly and framed his face in
her hands. "You have every intention of drawing up that
document and granting me immunity, correct?"

"Yes, but—"

"That's all I need to know. I *trust* you." Her gaze
narrowed ever so slightly. "Or is that not the problem?
Do you not trust me? Do you still think I could be involved in this with Bobby? Do you think this is some
ploy on my part to keep an eye on you, so I can report
what you've been up to?"

"Absolutely not. I wouldn't have made the agreement
with Emma, if I believed that," he assured her.

Her smile returned. "Then we don't have a problem,
do we?"

Rafe gave up the battle. "Actually we do," he told her.

She regarded him with a resigned expression. "What
now?"

"You have way too many clothes on, Ms. Petrillo."

It took a moment for his words to register, but when
they did, her expression brightened. "If only all of our
problems could be solved so easily," she said.

She reached for the hem of her T-shirt, but Rafe stilled
her hands. "In good time, Gina. In good time."

This time when his mouth found hers, there was no
hesitation, no restraint, just a slow, sweet, savoring kiss
that rocked him like nothing had in years. Knowing that
this time there would be no pulling back gave him permission to take his time and enjoy the trip. This time the
final destination was never in doubt.

Chapter Eleven

Rafe made love just exactly the way Gina had imagined he would, with total concentration and the kind of raw passion that had been missing from her life. His mouth was hot and clever, but his hands were positively wicked. Long, lazy caresses alternated with skimming, intimate touches that made her crave more. He did things to her breasts that made her cry out and arch toward him, pleading for him not to stop.

And then he skimmed away her sensible cotton panties and began yet another wicked exploration that had her writhing and begging for release.

"Not just yet," he whispered, his breath cool against the bare skin of her sensitive inner thigh.

He began a whole new assault of kisses that roved from stomach to ankle to toes and back again, until he reached the juncture of her thighs. When he touched her with his tongue, she came apart in a shuddering release.

Clutching his shoulders, she came slowly back to earth, then met his smoldering gaze. She felt a need to say something, to explain how devastating, how incredible the experience had been. "That was—"

"Just the beginning," he said, cutting off her words with a kiss that sent her senses soaring once more.

Her body was straining yet again by the time his gaze locked with hers. Poised above her, he reminded her of a proud warrior, a little arrogant, a lot masculine. She hadn't thought it was possible to want more than he'd already given her, but she did. Anticipation and yearning coupled with a building heat as he finally, at long last, entered her.

The sensation, the hard, slick slide of his arousal deep inside her took her breath away. But just beyond that incredible moment of satisfaction there was a hunger for more, a hunger that began with a sense of loss as he withdrew, then deepened as he entered her again.

The rhythm, as old as time, but new to her with this man became a torment and a pleasure. Rafe added nuances she'd never imagined, slow, fast, then slow again, teasing her, streaking toward a peak, then carrying her down, lulling her, before finally taking her to an impossible height, one that had every part of her at a fever pitch, demanding release, reaching for it.

They tumbled over the edge together, panting, clinging together, crying out in unison.

When the waves of pleasure had stilled, when heated flesh began to cool, she sighed deeply and buried her head against his neck. Then, cradled in his arms, feeling safer than she had in months, maybe even years, she slept. The very last thing on her mind was the future and what it might hold.

Rafe was a little awed, more than a little panicked by what had just happened between him and the woman who was curled so trustingly against him. He was not a man prone to making impulsive decisions. His relationships, such as they were, tended to be simple. He was definitely not a man who thought in terms of forever.

But here he was, completely sated and drained from making love with a woman who had impulsively thrown herself at him, who was about as complicated as anyone he'd ever met and who was definitely all about forever. How the hell had this happened?

Okay, he knew how it had happened. He'd been thinking about Gina in this way for weeks now. Maybe not from the moment they'd met, but certainly from the first time they'd kissed. Once the ethical barrier to pursuing a relationship had been lifted by that agreement he'd made earlier with Emma, he'd been all too susceptible.

He sighed and shifted until she was cradled even more tightly against him. Never one to transfer the blame for something to someone else when his own role was perfectly evident, he forced himself to accept responsibility for what had just happened. Gina might have initiated things, but he'd been an eager participant.

All of which begged the question, what now? If he had a functioning brain cell left, he'd leave the pursuit of Bobby Rinaldi in Emma's capable hands and hightail it back to New York and his other clients. Sticking around Winding River and carrying on a fling with Gina was a dead-end road for both of them. She would realize it once the initial physical attraction wore off. What was the expression? Their relationship was definitely too hot not to cool down. That was certainly his experience. Even relationships based on more than he and Gina had in common eventually burned themselves out. His mother's certainly had. In fact, he predicted that after today, now that he and Gina had tasted what had previously been forbidden, the attraction would be well on its way to dying.

He glanced at her, took in the rosy cheeks, the lush curve of breast and hip, the dark cloud of tousled hair, the thoroughly kissable mouth. His body stirred with all the urgency he had felt not a half hour before.

So much for diminishing attraction, he thought as he ran his hand over petal-soft skin that smelled of citrus and ginger. Her nipple peaked to a hard bud against his palm. She shifted restlessly as his caresses intensified and became bolder.

Then she was wide awake and moving against him, welcoming him, hips thrusting against hips, seeking, urgent. The heat climbed as he buried himself deep inside, withdrew, then sank into her again and again.

This time, she was the first to cry out, the first to reach a shuddering climax. As the waves washed through her, they set off his own explosion. Muscles bunched, strained, then relaxed into the demanding pleasure of it.

"Too much," she cried as their bodies mated with fierce intensity, arching together in another wild burst of sensation. Then, "More, please, more."

Her words were an echo of his reeling thoughts. Being with Gina was too much by far, and yet he knew, with soul-searing honesty, that he could never get enough.

When Gina woke from an exhausted sleep this time, there were no sneaky caresses teasing her awake. In fact she was in the king-size bed all alone. The sound of water running told her that Rafe was taking a shower. His side of the vast mattress was cool to her touch, suggesting that he'd been up for a while now.

It was dark outside. Inside, there was only the glow

from beneath the bathroom door and a digital clock on a bedside stand to light the room.

Gina heard the water shut off, the sound of off-key humming, and grinned. What would he think if she slipped into the room and joined him? Oddly, she felt more uncertain about his reaction now than she might have hours ago.

She had seduced Rafe. There was no question in her mind about that. She had done precisely what she'd told Emma she intended to do. She had wanted something and she had gone after it.

What now, though? Was Rafe happy about the turn of events? She knew he had enjoyed the sex as much as she had, but beyond that? Had all those doubts of his crowded in again? Had he succumbed to all of the sensible, rational arguments that would have kept her out of his bed in the first place? Not knowing kept her right where she was, waiting, feeling more vulnerable than she had in years.

Not that she regretted anything, not one single, amazing second. But it would be nice to know where she stood, what she could expect when he emerged from behind that door. She watched it with the same trepidation a suspect might feel awaiting a jury's verdict. Even as she made the analogy, she cringed.

When Rafe eventually opened the door, her heart slammed against her ribs. He was wearing a pair of still-new jeans and nothing more. The snap was undone and the waistband rode low on his hips. No cowboy had ever looked sexier than this. Longer now than when he'd first arrived in Winding River, his hair was damp and tousled. She wished she dared to run her fingers through it to add to its surprising tendency to curl. She gave him a hesitant smile, which he was a little too slow to return. Her pulse skittered unsteadily.

"You're awake," he said, his tone cautious and surprisingly uncertain.

"So are you," she noted, forcing a teasing note into her voice.

Looking incredibly unsettled and awkward, he dropped down on the side of the bed. He lifted his hand as if he might caress her, but then let it drop to his thigh.

"Are you okay?" he asked, studying her intently.

"Of course. Why wouldn't I be?"

"I thought you might be having second thoughts."

Her gaze searched his. "Are you?"

"Hell, yes," he said fiercely, but his expression softened to take the sting out. "And if you were the least bit sensible, you'd be scared spitless, too."

She grinned at that. "I don't scare so easily."

"We really do have to talk about this, Gina."

"Why? We're two consenting adults. Why do we need to make a big deal out of something so natural?"

"Because—"

She frowned at him. "I will not talk this to death, Rafe. I will not regret it. If that's what you're hoping for, forget it."

"I don't want you to regret it. I just want you to realize that it can't go on."

"And why is that? Because you have decreed that it can't?"

"No, because it can't go anywhere."

She began to lose patience with his oh-so-reasonable tone. "Why can't it? And who said I wanted it to go anywhere, anyway?"

"Let's face it, Gina. You don't do this sort of thing."

"Have sex?"

"Have *casual* sex," he corrected.

"And that's all you have," she shot back. "Is that what you're trying to tell me?"

He winced at the charge, but he didn't deny it.

"Well, that's just dandy," she said, taking his silence for assent. "We're agreed. This is casual sex. If I agree to those terms, I assume you'll have no objections." She gathered the sheet around her, dragged it off the bed and marched into the bathroom, spine rigid, shoulders back. She shot one last heated look over her shoulder. "Since this is all so damned casual, I don't expect you to buy me dinner. Give me ten minutes and I'll be out of here and you can get back to that paperwork."

Then she slammed the bathroom door behind her.

The roar of the shower drowned out her hot, salty tears. At least, she hoped it did. And if Rafe had a single shred of decency in his body, he would be gone when she came out.

Instead, as she leaned against the wall of the shower and let her tears flow, the curtain was suddenly yanked back. Still in his jeans, Rafe stepped into the shower with her, his expression grim and determined. She was too shocked to react.

Rafe tucked a finger under her chin and forced her to meet his gaze. His thumb brushed futilely at the mix of streaming tears and flowing water from the pounding shower. "I'm sorry," he said, looking contrite.

"For what?"

"For upsetting you. I was just trying to make sure that we were on the same page. I wasn't trying to diminish what had happened."

"But you did," she said, her voice catching. "You made it seem cheap and tawdry and unimportant."

He sighed, gathering her close. "It was anything but that. In fact, that's the problem. You caught me off guard.

I never expected to feel so much, to want so much, especially with things so uncertain.''

"What things? I thought everything between you and me was finally straightforward. You want Bobby. I agreed to help you in any way I can.''

"It's more than that, Gina. You have to see that.''

"I don't,'' she insisted. "You'll have to explain it.''

He pushed wet strands of hair back from her face, a smile tugging at his lips. "You want an explanation here? Now?''

"You picked the place,'' she pointed out.

"But there are so many more interesting things we could be doing,'' he said, his gaze drifting from mouth to breasts, then lower still.

Gina could see the hard bulge of his arousal pressing against soaking wet denim. When he ran a finger along the curve of her breast, then skimmed a nail across the peak, she shuddered. Desire, hot and urgent, slammed through her once more. All thoughts of resolving their differences fled as she reached for the zipper on his jeans, slid it slowly down, then took the hard thrust of his arousal in her hand.

Rafe moaned, then lifted her until she could straddle him, her back braced against the wall. There, with the shower cascading over them like a waterfall, their bodies slick and hot and hungry, they streaked toward a violent, earth-shattering climax that left them panting and clinging together.

When they could move again, when they had caught their breath, Rafe lowered her to unsteady legs, then reached for the soap and gently washed her. Then he cut off the water, reached for a towel and dried first her, then himself.

"Now then,'' he said, his tone sounding deliberately

casual. "What do you say we get dressed and go get some dinner?"

Gina knew what he was doing. He wanted to get them onto neutral turf before renewing the discussion of the future.

"I could call Tony's and have a pizza delivered right here," she suggested.

"Bad idea," he said at once.

"Why?"

"I seem to be having trouble keeping my hands to myself."

She regarded him with amusement. "And that's a problem because...?"

"Because I'm starving and you must be, too."

"A pizza would solve that," she said.

"So would a nice, quiet dinner in a restaurant where we'd be obligated to behave ourselves. We could have a little wine, a little pleasant conversation."

"Why do I think that the conversation you have in mind will be anything but pleasant?"

His jaw set stubbornly. "Gina—"

"Okay, say I agree to go out, will you agree not to bring up our relationship?"

He seemed to be torn, but he finally nodded.

"And no mention of Bobby?"

"Okay," he agreed with obvious reluctance. "What's left?"

She patted his cheek. "I'm sure we'll think of something. If not, we'll invite Tony and Francesca to join us. You can help me convince him to take her to Italy while I cover things here for him."

Rafe paused in pulling on a clean shirt to stare at her. "You're talking temporarily, right?"

"Yes. Why the resigned look?"

"Because I was hoping that now that we have this agreement, you'd be ready to go back to New York."

"If you're anxious to go home, go," she said, though her heart felt suddenly empty at the prospect of him leaving. "Emma or I will keep you posted if Bobby turns up."

Rafe shook his head. "Not that I don't trust you, but I'll feel better if I'm around to keep a close eye on you."

Something in his voice alarmed her. "Because you still don't trust me?"

"No, because we have no way of knowing whether Bobby took that money because he's desperate for some reason."

"Desperate? What on earth do you mean?"

"If he's gotten himself mixed up in something bad, something like gambling debts or big-time drug deals, he could be in danger. I don't want him dragging you into that."

The thought of there being any actual danger in all of this had never occurred to Gina. The prospect of losing Café Tuscany had been daunting enough.

"Surely, if there were any danger, he would warn me," she said slowly but without much conviction. After all, if Bobby had been concerned about her at all, he would never have put her in this position in the first place.

"We can't be sure of that," Rafe said, his expression grim.

He brushed a finger across her forehead. "Don't look so worried. I am not going to let anything happen to you."

He held out his hand. "Let's go. I recommend a big plate of pasta and some wine."

Gina sighed. Normally that was a prescription she would recommend herself. Tonight, though, she had a feeling it was going to take a whole lot more to chase away the sudden butterflies in her stomach.

She was still unnerved when they reached Tony's. Peg Lafferty, who'd been with Tony since he opened, led them to a table near the kitchen. "I know Tony's going to be running in and out to talk to you, so this will be more convenient."

"Where's Francesca tonight?" Gina asked.

"Home. She's not feeling well."

"What's wrong? Do you know?"

"I'm not sure," Peggy said, her expression filled with concern. "She's been staying home a lot lately. Tony doesn't talk much about it, and I haven't wanted to pry."

He hadn't said anything to Gina, either, but she had none of Peggy's reticence about prying. She intended to get to the bottom of this. "Tell him I'm here, okay?"

"Will do," Peggy promised. "Everyone's eating late tonight, it seems. He's got a half dozen orders going right now, but he'll be out soon. Can I bring you a bottle of Chianti while you look over the menu?"

"Chianti would be good," Rafe told her. When she had gone, he regarded Gina with concern. "Don't start taking what she said and exaggerating it in your head. Francesca may be perfectly fine. She might just be taking some time off."

"You don't know her. She doesn't take time off, not willingly." She started to stand up. "Maybe I should go over there to check on her."

Rafe tugged her back down. "Maybe you should wait and let Tony answer your questions before you go charging over to see her."

"These are my friends," she said, "not yours."

"That doesn't make my advice any less sensible," he said mildly.

Gina sighed and relented. "You're probably right. I'm probably making a mountain out of a molehill. Tony would have told me if it was anything serious."

"Exactly," he said just as Peggy returned with the wine and a promise that Tony would join them shortly.

"Do you want to order before that?" she asked.

"No," Gina said at once. "I want answers before I want food."

"Speak for yourself," Rafe said. "How about a plate of antipasto for the time being?"

"You've got it," Peggy said, then went off to check on another group of late arrivals.

When the antipasto arrived, Gina realized that she was ravenous. Since there was nothing she could do until Tony emerged from the kitchen, anyway, she picked up a carrot stick, then a stalk of celery, then reached for the warm garlic bread that Peggy had brought with it. Rafe watched her approvingly.

"That's better," he said at last. "You've got some color back in your cheeks. I was worried there for a bit. This tendency of yours to take on everyone else's problems is not a good thing."

"These are my friends," she said defensively. "What would you have me do?"

He sighed. "I imagine telling you to maintain a little distance would be a waste of my breath."

She studied his expression, trying to gauge if he was actually serious. "Can you do that? Can you maintain a nice, safe distance when your friends are in trouble?"

Her question seemed to catch him off guard. "Truthfully, there are not that many people I consider friends."

Gina stared at him. "Surely you can't mean that."

"It's true. I have business acquaintances. There are dozens of people at my law firm who are colleagues, but friends? People I'd call up just to go out and have a drink for the fun of it? I haven't had the time.''

"But that's awful," she said without thinking about her own barren social life in New York. Was she any better? "Everyone should have friends, people they can count on, people they would go the extra mile for without question.''

"Well, I don't.''

"Do you expect me to believe that there is no one important in your life?''

"That's the truth.''

"What about your mother? You said you jumped into this case because of her," she said triumphantly. "You must care about her.''

"I don't like to see anyone swindled. *That's* why I took the case.''

"I don't believe you.''

"It's true.''

Before she could probe any deeper, they were joined by Tony, who looked more tired than she had ever seen him. Rafe looked relieved to have her attention shifting away from him and on to Tony, but she had no intention of forgetting about his admission that there was no one in his life who really mattered to him.

"Are you okay?" Gina asked Tony.

"It's been a busy night. That's all," Tony said.

"Have you eaten?''

"I haven't had the time.''

Gina jumped up. "Then you sit right here. I'm going to fix something for all of us. And if anyone else comes in, I'll handle it. Have a glass of wine. Talk to Rafe. Relax.''

Tony patted her hand. "You're a good girl, *cara mia*.''

"And a better cook," she reminded him with a grin. "I'll make you two a meal that will make you weep."

Rafe started to protest, but Gina silenced him with a look. "I need to do this," she said quietly. "It won't take long."

"It will take as long as it takes," Tony chided, his expression stern. "Good food cannot be rushed."

Gina pressed a kiss to his pale cheek. "Advice from the master," she teased, managing to keep a smile plastered firmly on her face as she left the two men to their wine and their conversation.

But once she reached the kitchen, she sagged against the door. Something was terribly wrong. Suddenly her own problems with Bobby, her confusion over her relationship with Rafe, none of it mattered. How sad that Rafe didn't understand the meaning of such deep and abiding friendships.

But maybe, once she'd dealt with whatever was going on with Tony and Francesca, once Karen's life was settled again, maybe then she could take the time to teach him.

Chapter Twelve

Rafe studied Tony's tired face and concluded that Gina was right to be concerned. He might not know the man well, but there was a general air of despondency about him that was unmistakable even to him.

"Gina's worried about you," he said.

"And I am worried for her," Tony responded. "The longer this business with her partner drags on, the sadder she becomes. I don't like it. If I knew this man, I would wring his neck myself."

"Join the club," Rafe said, though he chafed at Tony's evasive change of topic. Apparently, he really was lousy at this friendship thing. Surely a man with his skills at cross-examination should have been able to get a direct response. He considered his words, realized then that unlike his courtroom style, he'd made a statement, rather than asking a probing question. It seemed like he was even out of practice at being a decent lawyer.

"But I wasn't really talking about Gina. I was asking about you. Is everything okay?" he asked more pointedly. "Peggy said something earlier about your wife that made Gina conclude that she might not be well."

If anything, Tony looked even more dispirited. "Francesca grows more homesick day by day. Her only sister, who lives in Rome, is not well. Francesca wishes she were there with her, but she refuses to go back to Italy alone, and I cannot simply close the business and leave."

"There is a solution," Rafe said thoughtfully, hating himself for even thinking of it, much less voicing it. He needed to get back to New York one of these days, though amazingly the pressure seemed to lessen with every day he spent right here in Wyoming with Gina. He was beginning to adapt to the slower pace and friendlier lifestyle. And except for court, he was able to keep up with most of his work. Lydia kept his fax machine humming, and what was too lengthy and complicated to be faxed she shipped overnight.

"Oh?" Tony said, his expression brightening hopefully. "What solution?"

"Let Gina take over. She's insistent on staying here for the time being because of her friend Karen. It would give her something to do."

Tony seemed startled by the suggestion. "Were you not the one who warned me not to expect her to work here again?"

"I meant permanently," Rafe said, then shrugged. "Who knows, though? Maybe I was wrong about that, as well. Gina is not an easy woman to read."

Tony looked shocked by the assessment. "Gina? She wears her heart on her sleeve. Anyone who knows her can see that."

"Then maybe I don't know her as well as I thought."

"Or perhaps as well as you would like to?" Tony inquired, looking amused. "Or is it that what you see terrifies you, so you pretend not to see it?"

Rafe glanced toward the kitchen, hoping to catch a glimpse of the woman in question, but the door remained steadfastly closed. "It's possible that you're right," he admitted, turning back to Tony. "Maybe I do see things that scare me, even though a part of me wants what she wants."

"This is a good thing," Tony said enthusiastically. "I am very pleased. Admitting what you want is always the first step."

"First step to what?" Rafe asked.

"The future." He grinned. "Now, what would you like to know about our Gina? Ask, and I will tell you."

His sudden openness startled Rafe. "Why the change of heart? You've been refusing to discuss her with me before now."

Tony's amusement seemed to grow. "Because you have changed. As has your reason for being here, I suspect. Now, tell me, what is it about Gina that you do not understand?"

Rafe asked the first thing that came to mind. "Is she a good chef?"

"Of all the things you might have asked, that is what you pick?" Tony said with a sad shake of his head. "Perhaps I was wrong about you, after all. I was expecting something personal."

"I thought cooking was personal to her. It's what she does."

"Yes," Tony agreed. "But not who she is. Besides, I cannot believe you have never eaten in her restaurant."

"Never, though my business associates dine there all

the time.'' Rafe thought of Lydia and added, ''And my secretary loves the place.''

''Because Gina has a passion for food. She understands it. She knows what will add to a meal and what will distract. She shares all of that when she cooks.''

''Then why hasn't she fought harder to keep Café Tuscany afloat? I know she came here for that reunion, but I thought she would go back at once and charge into battle to save the restaurant. Instead, there have been times when I've had to wonder if she even cares whether it closes or not.''

Tony looked shocked by Rafe's assessment. ''You are wrong,'' he said fiercely. ''She cares, too much perhaps. She has tried to distance herself, I think, out of fear. She is trying not to let it matter, in case she is not able to keep it open.''

When Rafe would have responded, Tony stopped him with a sign. ''Wait, there is more. There is one thing that matters more to Gina than food.''

''Her friends,'' Rafe guessed.

Tony gave a curt nod of satisfaction. ''Precisely. And can you see how that has affected what she'd done these past weeks? She has taken their burdens as her own, but she has not shared hers with them.''

''And she has stayed on because she cares about her friend Karen,'' Rafe said slowly. ''She will stay on longer because of you and Francesca. If there is another friend with another crisis, she will extend her stay yet again.''

''True, but it is more than that. She has stayed because a man she trusted, a man she believed in and counted on, betrayed her. Bobby Rinaldi is a criminal to you, but to Gina he was a friend. Think about that,'' Tony said quietly. ''I will go and get us another bottle of wine.''

He left Rafe feeling shaken. Not once had he stopped

to consider the impact Bobby's actions would have had on Gina emotionally. He'd thought only in terms of dollars and cents, only in terms of the business, not the friendship, quite likely because he had never established such deep ties to another person.

Of course Gina had been devastated. To the woman Tony had described—the woman Rafe was only beginning to know—losing a friend would be far worse than losing a restaurant.

Rafe wasn't entirely sure he could understand that depth of feeling for another person. He didn't profess to understand love, either, and this was something altogether different, something he'd always assumed would be less intense, less demanding.

In his world, there were no messy, emotional connections. No long-term lovers. As he had explained to Gina, there were colleagues, business associates, casual acquaintances. Even his relationship with his mother was coolly polite, rather than loving. He'd grown too jaded over the years, first by watching his parents' marriage disintegrate, later by watching criminals—and yes, his colleagues, too—manipulate the legal system.

But when he thought of the way Lauren had rushed to Gina's defense while knowing none of the facts, when he considered how Emma was prepared to staunchly defend Gina, he could see that there were people in the world to whom loyalty and friendship were more than mere words.

A part of him wanted that kind of closeness to another human being—to Gina—but he was afraid to risk it. People who made commitments risked betrayal and hurt. He had only to look at what Bobby had done to Gina to see that.

And yet never, not even once, had he had the sense that Gina regretted her friendship with Rinaldi, only that it had come to this tragic end. Though she had never said the words, he realized that was also why she had been so slow to join forces with him, so reluctant to leap to her own defense and throw Bobby to the wolves. She hadn't been ready to give up on her friend.

Rafe wondered wistfully what it would be like to be deserving of that kind of loyalty. Bobby certainly wasn't. Was Rafe? He thought of what could still happen to take Café Tuscany away from Gina. He had set those wheels in motion with his suit against the restaurant and Rinaldi. Would Gina ultimately blame him for that, especially if it cost her the business she had poured her heart and soul into? Would she hate him for it? Or would she understand and forgive?

Time would tell, he supposed, then he shuddered at the thought. It implied far more patience than he had. But what choice did he have? None. Professionally and personally, he was going to have to see this through on whatever timetable it took. He tried to see beyond that to the future, but to his frustration it was disturbingly blank.

"Sorry I took so long," Gina said, sliding a plate of steaming lasagna in front of him. "This is Francesca's favorite, and it took a while to get all the ingredients together. I sent some home to her with Tony."

"Did he tell you about her homesickness?" he asked, amazingly unsurprised that Gina had thought of preparing Francesca's favorite dish.

She nodded. "I told him to take her to Italy, that I would cover for him."

Rafe grinned, pleased that his estimation of her reaction had been proved right. "I told him you would do that."

She regarded him with surprise. "Did you? Do you approve, especially since it means another delay in getting back to New York?"

"You weren't prepared to go anytime soon, anyway. I'd accepted that."

"But you're not happy about it, are you?"

He lifted her hand and pressed a kiss to her knuckles. "Sticking around here for the time being is who you are. Since I seem to like who you are more and more, how can I possibly argue with your decision?"

"A wise man," she said approvingly.

"Not so wise," he said, tucking her hand against his thigh. "But I'm getting there."

There were a half dozen messages for Rafe when he returned to his hotel room. He checked them while Gina retreated to her own room next door, the room she had insisted on booking even after he'd said she could stay with him.

"Not here, where my parents will hear about it," she had told him.

"Do you honestly think being next door will be much of an improvement? People will draw whatever conclusions they want anyway."

"Maybe so, but at least I can tell them that we are not living together in plain sight of all their neighbors."

He'd been forced to accept her reasoning. At the moment he was grateful since two of the messages were from Lydia, who sounded increasingly amused by the fact that he was still in Winding River. Calling her back with Gina in the room would have been a test of his ability to lie with a straight face.

Another message was from his paralegal, Joan Lansing, and one was from his investigator reporting that there was a trail suggesting Bobby Rinaldi might be in the Cayman Islands.

"Let me know what you want me to do," the man

concluded. "I could use a free trip down there. I have some scuba gear I've been dying to try out."

Rafe glanced up at the end of the message and saw Gina staring at him, her expression frozen.

"Bobby's in the Cayman Islands?" she asked, looking oddly shaken.

"Could be."

"Are you sending that man after him?"

Rafe couldn't read her tone at all. "What do you want me to do?"

She blinked in surprise. "You're asking me?"

"That's what it sounded like," he said lightly. "What do you want, Gina? Do you want him caught? Do you want all of this resolved once and for all?"

"Of course I want him caught," she snapped, then sighed. "Then again, a part of me keeps trying to pretend he's down there on some impromptu vacation and that he'll come back on his own."

"You know him better than I do," Rafe said. "Is there a chance of that?"

For a long time he thought she might not answer. There was no mistaking the misery in her eyes, the uncertainty.

"I don't know," she whispered at last. "I honestly don't think I ever knew him at all."

Thinking of what Tony had said earlier, Rafe told her, "I know I accused you of lousy judgment in going into a partnership with him, but what happened isn't your fault. You saw what he wanted you to see, a charming man who was good at getting people to trust him, good at finding backers for the restaurant. You're not the only person he took in, sweetheart. My mother is older and should be wiser, but she trusted him. So did many others, many of them supposedly savvy businessmen."

His words didn't seem to console her. She stared at him bleakly. "What do I do, Rafe?"

"Do you want Café Tuscany?"

"Yes," she said at once.

"Enough to go back right now and fight for it?"

Her expression faltered at that. "I can't. Karen, Tony, they're depending on me."

"They would understand," he said, knowing it was true of Tony and just as certain that Karen, whom he barely knew, would feel the same way because she loved Gina, as did all her other friends.

"I suppose. But this trip is so important to Francesca. I can't go back on my word."

He studied her intently. "And there's a part of you that's happy here, isn't there?" he asked with sudden insight. "There's a part of you that is glad to have the chance to cook for friends and family, rather than anonymous strangers."

"I hadn't really thought about it, but yes," she said slowly. "I'm looking forward to being back in Tony's kitchen, to having time, even on a busy night, to sit for a minute with my friends while they try some recipe I've been experimenting with."

"Do you think that feeling is just temporary?" he asked with an astonishing sense of dread.

"I honestly don't know. I only know that right now this is where I want to be, where I *have* to be."

"And Rinaldi?"

"Tell your man to find him. No matter what I decide for myself, the investors and our vendors need to be paid. We owe them that."

Rafe nodded. "I'll call the investigator right now."

He woke the man from a sound sleep, told him to book that trip to the Cayman Islands, but to leave his scuba gear at home. "You won't have time for it. Find Rinaldi. See if he still has any of the money. Then we'll see where we go next."

"If Bobby is there, can you force him to come back?" Gina asked after he'd hung up. "Isn't that one of the places with no extradition agreement with the United States?"

"Yes, but I'm sure he can be *enticed* back, one way or another. First things first. Let's make sure that's where he is."

"Will you stay here while you wait or will you go back to New York?"

He ought to go straight back to New York. There was no real reason to keep Gina under surveillance, certainly no reason he had to do it himself. But for a whole lot of very confusing and conflicting reasons, he wanted to stay right here.

"What do you want me to do?" he asked, unhappy about this unexpected reluctance to leave. He'd come here a driven workaholic. He'd changed and he wasn't at all certain it was for the better.

Again Gina seemed startled that he was asking her preference. Then a smile spread slowly across her face. "Right now, I want you to forget about going anywhere and to come over here."

His heartbeat kicked up at the invitation in her eyes. "Oh? What did you have in mind?"

"If you don't know, then you're not half as brilliant as people think you are."

Rafe didn't hesitate. He took a few steps in her direction, but she met him halfway. When it came to being brilliant and clever, it turned out that Gina was no slouch herself. Her plans for the rest of the evening were far more innovative and satisfying than discussing the pros and cons of a return to New York. It also gave him a whole lot more to consider the next time the prospect of leaving Wyoming came up.

Gina was still half-asleep in Rafe's arms when the phone in her room rang. She leaped and ran to answer it. The sound of Bobby's voice snapped her awake.

"Bobby, where the hell are you?"

"If you think I'm going to tell you that, now that I know you've aligned yourself with the enemy, you're crazy."

"Why do you say that?"

"You're at the same hotel. Your parents told me where to find you. Are you sleeping with him?" he asked.

She ignored the question. "Why are you calling?"

"To tell you that chasing me down won't do you a bit of good. I'm safe."

"In the Caymans?" she asked.

From the other room she heard Rafe groan. She realized she had just given away their tactical advantage in finding Bobby.

"Why would you think I'm in the Caymans?" Bobby asked suspiciously. "You've got someone following me, haven't you?"

"Well, what did you expect?" she retorted, losing patience with him, with all of it. "You took off with the company money, ripped off our suppliers and investors. Of course you're being followed. If you have a grain of sense left in that pea brain of yours, you'll come home on your own and face the music before this gets any worse."

"It can't get any worse," he said. "Not back there, anyway. Down here I can live like a king."

She figured that was the final admission that they'd guessed right about where he was.

"Only if you can ignore your conscience," she said.

He laughed at that. "Not a problem."

"Just tell me one thing," she said. "Why did you do it? I thought we were friends."

"We were, doll. But friendship has its limits. In the end you have to look out for number one."

"That's a terrible way to live."

"No, that's the *only* way to live. Survival," he said succinctly. "That's what it's all about. Now, do me a favor."

"What? After everything you've done, you expect me to do you a favor?"

"Let's just say it's in your own best interests."

"Why is that?"

"If you call off whoever's tailing me, then I'll send you a little something to help pay off the debts. If business is still booming, you ought to be able to survive this little bump in the road. One day you might even thank me for turning a thriving business over to you."

"And if I don't?"

"You won't get a dime, and whoever shows up looking for me will run into some serious trouble down here. Gotta go, girl. You take care of yourself," he said, then laughed. "And I mean that sincerely. Nobody else will do it for you."

He hung up before she could respond. She was trembling when Rafe appeared and took the receiver from her hand. He replaced it, then took her in his arms.

"Are you okay? Come back to bed."

She went with him. "He threatened to do something to your investigator." She stared at Rafe, still struggling with shock at Bobby's cool demeanor and menacing threat. "He meant it, too. I could hear it in his voice. You need to call your man back."

"Flynn can take care of himself. He's dealt with bigger threats than Rinaldi. Did he confirm that he's in the Caymans?"

She nodded. "I had no idea he could be so cold, that he could be so totally self-involved."

"What else did he say?"

"That if I called off whoever was tailing him, he'd send me money to pay off some of the debts. He sounded as if that were such a magnanimous gesture on his part. He *owes* those people. He *owes* me."

Rafe chuckled.

"What's so damned funny?"

"It's good to see you getting angry," he said.

"I've been angry," she retorted.

"But not at Bobby," he suggested mildly.

"Of course I've been mad at Bobby," she said, confused by the suggestion.

Rafe shook his head. "Most of the time you've been mad at me."

She started to argue, then realized he was right. She'd been furious at Rafe for following her to Wyoming, for being suspicious of her, when it was Bobby who'd put her in that position.

She hadn't wanted to be mad at Bobby. She'd wanted to understand why her friend had done something so irresponsible, so criminal. She'd been upset by Rafe's distrust, because a part of her recognized that she should have been more suspicious of Bobby from the beginning. She'd seen how glib he could be, how little he took seriously. Maybe she should even have seen all of this coming.

"I was wrong," she said eventually. "You had no

choice but to come after me, to keep an eye on me. I used terrible judgment, about Bobby, about running away, about everything.''

He tucked a finger under her chin. ''Hey, don't be so hard on yourself. The man's a con artist. He took you in, the same as he did everyone else.''

Rafe's reassurances didn't soothe her at all. The only thing that helped when her mind was whirling was work. She left the warmth of Rafe's bed.

''I have to go.''

''Where?''

''To Tony's. If you need me, you'll find me there.''

''In the middle of the night?''

She shrugged as if the hour were unimportant. ''I'll get some baking done for tomorrow.''

To her relief, beyond that initial token protest, he didn't try to stop her.

Funny, she thought, as she raced through her shower, dressed and went to work. She was beginning to think that maybe Rafe understood her better after a few weeks than she understood herself after twenty-eight years.

Chapter Thirteen

"So, boss, are you ever coming back here?" Lydia inquired, her voice threaded with that superior amusement that Rafe found so annoying. "Not that I'm complaining, mind you. It's been really, really peaceful with you away, but the partners are beginning to ask whether you still work here. Your billable hours lately are the pits."

"Not so," Rafe protested, his gaze drifting to the bed with its tangle of sheets. Gina had left it far too soon last night, though after her conversation with Rinaldi, Rafe had understood her need to be alone, to bury herself in the kind of work that gave her solace.

"Then where are your billing records?" Lydia asked, snapping his attention back to the harsh reality of dollars and cents that for years now had controlled way too much of how he spent his time.

"I'll pull them together and fax them later today."

"They were due yesterday," she pointed out. "You're

never late. Or at least you never were before you found a distraction like Gina Petrillo.''

"I thought this was exactly what you wanted when you let her cancel that appointment. You did have an ulterior motive, didn't you? You wanted me to chase after her. You were hoping that I'd be attracted to her.''

For a moment his comment was greeted with stunned silence. It wasn't often that Rafe could render Lydia speechless. He savored the moment.

"Are you saying what I think you're saying?" she asked eventually. "You're finally paying serious attention to someone?''

"I don't know how serious it is, but I am definitely paying attention," he admitted reluctantly.

"Well, hallelujah! Forget the billing report. I can do it myself.''

"You cannot fake a billing report," he scolded.

"Of course not," she said indignantly. "But I ought to know how you've been spending your time—at least some of it. I am the one who sends your work out there and answers your phone and relays your messages. I'll bet I could come pretty darn close to getting it right.''

Rafe decided to challenge her, though he was pretty sure she was right. Lydia was an extremely efficient woman who paid great attention to detail. "How many contracts do I have on my desk right now?''

"Thirty," she said at once. "I overnighted them to you yesterday. And you were on the phone at least three hours yesterday working on the Jackson-Waller electronics merger.''

"Five," he retorted firmly. "Not three, five.''

"Did you do any other work yesterday that I don't know about?''

"Not officially," he conceded. "I'm not billing my mother, remember?"

"Ah, so the rest of the time you were concentrating on Gina?" she said, managing to lace the suggestion with innuendo. "I guess we can't bill for *that,* can we?"

"You don't have to make it sound as if we were wrestling around naked in the mud."

"Is that how it sounded?" Lydia chuckled gleefully. "You sound a little defensive, boss. Why is that? Nobody expects you to put in twelve-hour days. There's nothing wrong with taking a little time out for dinner. Maybe a little socializing. Have you been doing more than that? Is your conscience bothering you?"

"Don't smart-mouth me," he grumbled.

"So, tell me," she began in a confiding tone that sounded a bit like a reporter for some sleazy tabloid, "have you slept with Gina yet?"

He wasn't nearly as shocked by the question as he probably should have been, but he absolutely, positively refused to be drawn into that particular discussion. He ignored the question and remained stubbornly silent.

"Not talking, huh?" Lydia said smugly. "I guess I can draw my own conclusions."

"Just keep your theories to yourself. And get me the file on the Whitney case. I'll need it in the morning. Joel Whitney—"

Lydia interrupted. "Mr. Whitney called yesterday with one of his usual inane questions that he could have answered himself if he knew how to read the contracts he signed. I've already put it in the mail."

Rafe laughed. "Okay, okay, you're the best secretary in the entire universe."

"Yes, I am," she agreed with no hint of false modesty. "You know, though, these expenses for moving every piece of paper in your office from New York to Wyoming are adding up. Ever thought of just staying there and transferring all the files? A moving van might be cheaper in the long run. And I hear Wyoming is great for skiing in the winter.''

"I don't ski. Why would I want to stay in Wyoming?''

''Because of a certain chef.''

''Who owns a restaurant in New York,'' he reminded her, vaguely disgruntled by the suggestion that he might be stuck in Wyoming forever if he wanted to be with Gina. "She'll be back, Lydia. So will I.''

''Whatever you say, boss.''

Rafe seriously doubted that, but he hung up, grateful to have gotten the woman's docile cooperation just this once, even if it had been feigned.

He leaned back in his chair and stared out the window. Summer was winding down. The observation startled him. He'd been here way too long, if he could tell just from glancing outside that the seasons were changing. The slant of the sun was different, the intensity of the heat had lessened. He opened his appointment book, looked at a calendar and realized he'd been here for over two months, from the end of June to the beginning of September. Moreover, he hadn't gone completely stir crazy. Far from it.

He looked at that pile of contracts sitting on his desk, weighed those against the chance to catch a glimpse of Gina and stood up. To soothe his guilty conscience, he stuffed several contracts in his briefcase and headed for Tony's. If there wasn't a law against working away from New York, then there certainly wasn't one preventing him from working at a restaurant table. Half the lawyers he knew conducted their business over lunch. Of course, most of them were with their clients or an opposing counsel.

The only companion he was hoping for was Gina.

Gina was so exhausted from her overnight work-a-thon she could barely see straight and the lunch hours were just getting started. Fortunately, most weekdays Tony's was fairly slow at midday. A few people came in for pizza, a few for his stromboli or meatball sandwiches, but the real rush didn't start till evening. The prospect of sneaking back to the hotel for a nap was the only thing keeping her going.

She was sitting at the island which doubled as a chopping block, her chin resting in her hands, her eyes half-closed when Peggy came in to announce that Rafe was in the dining room.

"He wants to see you, if you're not too busy," she told Gina. "Since there's not another paying customer in the place yet, I told him you'd be right out."

For a moment Gina's heart leaped at the prospect of seeing Rafe, but during the long night when she'd been baking cannoli shells and preparing tiramisu for today's dessert specials, she'd spent a lot of time thinking about their relationship. She'd managed to convince herself it was doomed.

When she got back to New York—if she went back to New York—she was going to be faced with long hours and an uphill struggle to get Café Tuscany back into the black. She already knew that Rafe had been a workaholic. Neither of them would have ten seconds to spare once they resumed their old routines.

Relationships required nurturing. In the distant past that had been something at which she had excelled. In recent years she hadn't had time for it, not until she'd come back

to Wyoming and inadvertently found her priorities shifting back to the way they had once been. Despite the turmoil of recent weeks, her life felt more balanced now.
She could actually envision a time when she might be
perfectly contented to work right here, alongside Tony,
surrounded by the people who meant the most to her—
her family and friends. When she tried to add Rafe to that
image, she couldn't.

She glanced up and realized Peggy was regarding her
with puzzlement. "What?"

"If I had a guy who looked like him waiting for me, I
wouldn't be sitting in here with such a glum expression,"
Peggy said.

"You're absolutely right," Gina said, forcing a smile
and heading for the dining room. Hiding in the kitchen
was no way to deal with this. She needed to tell Rafe
about the conclusion she'd reached. Surely he wouldn't
be all that unhappy if she suggested that he go back to
New York.

Unfortunately, Rafe looked as if he was here to stay,
she noted as she spotted him sitting at a table beside a
window, papers spread out around him. He seemed perfectly content with his office away from home. She
walked over to join him.

"If you're going to set up an office in here, I'll have
to charge you rent," she said.

Rafe's gaze shot up, instantly filling with so much heat
it almost took her breath away. Why had she ever left the
man's room the night before? If this thing between them
was destined to end, why wasn't she taking advantage of
every single second it lasted?

"You look beat," he said, worry crowding out the desire in his expression.

"Just what every woman wants to hear. You need to work on your technique for flattery," she retorted.

"Your beauty is a given. You still look tired."

She grinned at that. "Better. But I'd suggest you keep practicing or you'll never get the girl."

A smile tugged at his lips. "I thought I already had the girl."

Her pulse did a little bump at that. "Oh, really?"

"Do I?"

She pulled out a chair and sat down. "Maybe," she said thoughtfully. "For the time being. In fact, we ought to talk about that."

"Uh-oh," he said. "You've had too much time to think overnight, haven't you?"

"I didn't spend it all on you," she said testily. "But when you did happen to cross my mind, it occurred to me that this is crazy."

"What's crazy?" he asked.

"This," she said, gesturing from him to herself and back. "You and me."

"Why is it crazy? You're the one who insisted on taking it to a whole new level. I'm just starting to get used to the idea. In fact, I'm just about convinced you're a genius."

"I don't think you're supposed to have to get used to the idea of caring about somebody. It's supposed to just happen."

"Not to me."

A tight note in his voice suggested he was admitting something to her that he rarely admitted, perhaps even to himself.

"You said something like that last night, but I can't believe it. You've never cared about someone?" she asked, unable to hide her incredulity. "Never?"

"Not really."

"What about your mother?"

"I told you, we maintain a polite distance."

Gina found the response appalling, but because of his forbidding expression, she let it go. "But you have been involved with a lot of women, right?"

"I've dated. I wouldn't say I've been 'involved' with any of them." He regarded her defensively. "Do we have to talk about this?"

"I think we do. Rafe, where do you see this going?"

"I don't know." His gaze locked with hers. "Do you?"

Gina sighed. "No," she said, then waved off the response as if to erase it. The truth was she had thought of little else all night long and she had vowed not ten minutes ago to be honest with him about her conclusions. "I take that back. If I'm being totally honest, I don't see it going anywhere. Not in the long term, at any rate."

His jaw tightened. "I see. May I ask why?"

She leaned forward. "Look, you and I didn't get off on the best foot at the beginning. You thought I was a criminal, for heaven's sake. Because of my past—no, just on general principle—I resented that like crazy. But there was this undeniable physical attraction between us even then. It was probably heightened because there was nothing we could do about it under the circumstances."

"But we did do something about it," he pointed out. "We made love."

"We had sex," she insisted. "And it was great. Fabulous, in fact."

"Glad to hear we were on the same page about that, at least," he retorted.

She refused to be intimidated by his sarcasm. "You

asked me why I thought it wouldn't work. I'm trying to tell you."

Rafe held up his hands. "By all means, though I'm not so sure we ought to be having a discussion about sex with half the town listening in."

"Half the town?" Gina echoed, then turned in her chair to find that the restaurant had begun to fill up. Several fascinated gazes were turned in their direction. She was going to kill Rafe for not warning her sooner. Or maybe Peggy, who was just passing by with a smirk on her face. Gina snagged her hand. "Why didn't you tell me we had customers?"

"You were sitting right here. I figured you weren't either blind or deaf," Peggy responded with an unrepentant grin. "I guess something else had captured your attention."

"Have you taken their orders?" she asked, barely resisting the desire to grind her teeth in frustration.

"I'm doing that right now," Peggy said cheerfully. "Everybody's been pretty happy just to watch the floor show."

Gina caught the amusement in Rafe's eyes just then. "Don't say another word," she told him. "And don't go anywhere. This conversation is not over."

He gave her a mock salute. "Take your time. I'll be right here." He winked at Peggy. "Bring me a glass of Chianti when you have a minute, okay?"

"You've got it," Peggy said. "It's on the house. I haven't had this much fun around here in ages. By comparison, Tony and Francesca are totally boring."

"You can't give away wine," Gina snapped, losing patience with the pair of them and their amusement at her expense.

"I'll pay for it out of my tips," Peggy said. "Something tells me they're going to be real good today."

Gina bit back the desire to respond and headed for the kitchen. It was too bad she'd done all the chopping and dicing earlier. Right now the prospect of slamming a really sharp knife down into something and cutting it to shreds held a whole lot of appeal.

It was more than two hours before she got back to Rafe. In addition to all the customers who'd seemingly been drawn in by reports of the lively discussion she and Rafe had been engaged in earlier, Karen had appeared, looking downcast and confused. She had been joined by Lauren and Emma. All three of them had regarded Gina with curiosity when she had emerged from the kitchen.

"Maybe you'd better sit down here and tell us what's going on," Emma advised. "Why are you working here?"

"Tony needed to take Francesca to Italy. I'm filling in."

"For how long?" Karen asked.

"I'm not sure."

"Are you thinking of staying here permanently?" Emma asked. "If so, we need to talk. It would change certain things."

Lauren, who was back in town again, immediately picked up on Emma's circumspect choice of words. "What things?" she asked. "I can totally understand if Gina wants to stay here."

All three of them stared at the glamorous superstar, whose visits were more and more frequent. They had assumed it was because of Karen. Now Gina wasn't so sure.

"You can?" Gina said.

"Well, of course I can," Lauren responded. "Wherever

we go, this is still home. Why wouldn't we want to come back? It's like a safe haven.''

Gina stared at her. "Why would *you* need a safe haven? Has something happened we don't know about?''

"No, of course not," Lauren said impatiently. "I was just saying that if we needed one, this is the place we'd be most likely to come.''

That said, she leaned toward Gina and asked in a conspiratorial tone, "So, is it true?''

Gina's composure slipped. "Is what true?'' she asked, even though she was pretty sure she knew precisely what was coming.

Lauren glanced pointedly across the room. "Were you and Rafe having a very public discussion about the fabulous sex you've been having?''

"Not intentionally,'' Gina said, though she could feel the embarrassed heat climbing into her cheeks.

"But you were talking about it?'' Lauren persisted. "There has been sex and it has been fabulous?''

"Yes,'' Gina admitted. "And a few people might have overheard. I thought we were alone.''

The other three exchanged glances.

"Interesting,'' Karen said, grinning.

"Isn't it, though,'' Lauren added.

"I thought I told you to stay away from him,'' Emma said. But despite the disapproval in her tone, her eyes were glinting with amusement.

Karen and Lauren turned to Emma. "Why would you tell her that?'' Lauren asked.

"Because it's inadvisable for the two of them to get mixed up at this particular moment in time,'' Emma said, again being very circumspect.

"Why?'' Lauren repeated. "Is he in the middle of a messy divorce or something?''

"Of course not," Gina said. "Rafe has never been married."

"Then I don't get it," Lauren said. "He's gorgeous. He's interested." Suddenly her enthusiastic expression faded. "But when he came here, he was after something. A deposition, wasn't it? That's why Emma objects to you seeing him."

"I am not going to talk about this," Gina said. "The deposition is no longer an issue. We're *partners*," she reminded Emma.

"I don't have that paper," Emma said.

Gina waved that off as a technicality. "It's a moot point anyway. Rafe and I are not an issue. *That's* what we were discussing when half the town decided to eavesdrop, then spread the word."

"I'm confused," Karen said. "The two of you are having fabulous sex, over Emma's objections, but you're not going to keep on seeing each other. Have I got that right?"

"Pretty much," Gina said.

"Is Emma the reason you're splitting up, then?" Karen asked.

"No," Gina said. "There is nothing to split up. There is no relationship."

"Just that fabulous sex," Lauren said, a gleam in her eyes. "I'm beginning to get it."

Karen stared at her. "You are? Explain it to me."

Lauren nodded. "Happily. Our friend Gina is running scared. For the first time in her life, she is attracted to a man who might mean more to her than preparing succulent feasts for strangers. Her priorities are all topsy-turvy, after years and years of knowing exactly what she wanted. What better way to fix things than to get rid of the distraction?"

Gina listened to the explanation first with indignation, then with dawning shock. Was Lauren right? Was that what she'd been doing—running scared because Rafe had been a threat to her goals? Obviously it was true that he'd been a threat when he'd first come to town. But that issue was all but dead, and he still posed a very real threat. She was beginning to want him a little too much, to want what they had together. Hell, she had all but thrown herself at him, she wanted him so badly.

"Well?" Lauren demanded, poking her in the ribs with an elbow. "How did I do? Am I good or what?"

"You're good," Gina admitted slowly. "Just one question. Now that you've psychoanalyzed me and nailed it, what the heck am I supposed to do about it?"

Chapter Fourteen

Rafe watched Gina and her friends across the room with a sinking sensation in the pit of his stomach. From the surreptitious glances being cast his way, he suspected he was the prime topic on the agenda. He wasn't sure how he felt about his fate being decided by women he barely knew. Would they encourage Gina to let this relationship play out or would they warn her away? As skittish as she clearly was, it wouldn't take much to ruin things for the two of them.

When he could stand it no longer, he stood up and crossed the restaurant. "You ladies look as if you're enjoying yourselves," he said, then tucked a hand under Gina's elbow. "Mind if I steal her away from you, though? We were in the middle of a conversation earlier. We need to finish it."

"Not now," Gina said, refusing to budge. "We can finish it later."

Rafe shook his head. "Something tells me now would be better. Excuse us, ladies."

Rafe tried to pull her up, but Gina held back. "I am visiting with my friends," she said, regarding him with mounting fury flashing in her eyes.

"I'm sure they won't object," he repeated confidently, giving each of them his most charming smile, the one that lulled witnesses into believing he was on their side.

"Will you?" he asked, all but daring any of them to protest.

When Emma started to reply, Lauren gave her a sharp nudge. "We don't mind at all," Lauren assured him. "I'm sure what you have to say is really, really important."

Gina scowled at her. "It's not that important," she grumbled. "It could wait."

Lauren beamed at her. "No, it can't. Just remember what I said."

Exhaling a deep sigh, Gina stopped fighting him then and stood up. She shrugged off his hand, but she did follow him back to his table.

"Would you care for a glass of wine?" Rafe asked when she was seated.

"No, thank you," she said a little too politely, her hands folded primly in front of her on the table, her gaze averted.

He refused to let her attitude get to him. "So, what did Lauren tell you?"

"Nothing that matters."

"She seemed to think otherwise. Come on, Gina," he coaxed. "What did she say? It had to do with us, didn't it?"

She leveled a withering look at him. "It did, but she

was wrong, flat-out, positively wrong. If I didn't believe that before, I do now.''

"Oh?''

Sparks lit her eyes. "I don't like being manhandled, Rafe.''

For a minute he was about to laugh, but her expression suggested she was dead serious. "Is that how you see it? You think I manhandled you just now?''

"You dragged me away from my friends over my objections. What would you call it?''

He thought back over everything that had happened in the last ten minutes. He was pretty sure she had come along willingly if not enthusiastically, but then again, he was a mere male. What did he know about finesse?

"Manhandling implies more physical force than I used,'' he protested.

"Okay, you bullied me into coming with you. Is that better?''

Rafe winced. "Not really. And if that's the way you see it, then I apologize. I was just trying to get back to a conversation that I thought was really important to both of us.''

She didn't seem appeased by the apology. Either she didn't take it seriously or there was something else entirely going on. He suspected it was the latter. "Is that really what has you upset with me, the fact that I interrupted your time with your friends?''

She looked vaguely disconcerted by the question, as if she hadn't expected him to guess that she was trying to sidestep the real problem. He watched her and waited.

"No,'' she said finally. "It's not that.''

"What then?''

"You came over just when I was trying to get the answer to a question.''

Rafe regarded her with confusion. "And?"

"I really wanted to know the answer," she said. "Isn't that obvious?"

"Ask me. Maybe I can answer it."

She chuckled, her expression wry. "I don't think so."

"Why not?"

"Because you're the problem. Well, not you," she corrected. "Me, and how I feel about you. The two of us. Together. Or not." She frowned at him. "See, it's very confusing."

Rafe was beginning to feel considerably better, but he was wise enough not to show it. "Okay. What is it you find most disturbing about us?"

"The fact that I care about you," she said, looking miserable. "Lauren accused me of running scared and, as much as I hate to admit it, she was right. I know I was the one who came on to you and all but dragged you into bed, but I didn't expect the sex to be so..."

"Fabulous?" he suggested, allowing himself a faint smile.

"Okay, yes," she admitted grudgingly. "I didn't expect it to be great and I didn't expect it to matter. I didn't expect *you* to matter."

The explanation filled in the rest of the picture. "And you were hoping your friends would clarify things, help you figure out what to do about that," he guessed.

"Exactly."

"It's just as well I dragged you away when I did then," he said.

She seemed thoroughly taken aback by his claim. "How can you say that?"

"Because they can't answer that," he told her, then held up his hand when she seemed to be about to speak. "I can't answer it, either. You're the only one who can figure out what your feelings are and what's best for you. Sorry, sweetheart, but I think we're going to have to muddle through this entirely on our own.''

She was already shaking her head by the time he finished. ''But I can't,'' she said. ''Not with you here, not with everything else that's going on. I can't think. My head is spinning.''

''Is there some reason why you have to decide all of this today?'' he asked.

''No, not really, but I hate this uncertainty. Everything in my life is up in the air.''

Rafe stood up, tugged his chair around to her side of the table then sat next to her. He cupped her face in his hands, his gaze locked with hers. The turmoil made her eyes darker than ever. His gaze shifted to her lips, but despite the temptation he resisted the desire to kiss her until she forgot all about her confusion.

''Okay, let's deal with one thing at a time. I'm no expert on relationships,'' he said quietly. ''We've established that, but I think this is one of those things you're not supposed to think about, Gina. You're supposed to go with your gut, with what you're feeling in here.'' He tapped her in the center of her chest. ''You said as much yourself earlier, remember?''

''But that's just it,'' she said wearily. ''I don't know what's in my heart. How can I? First Bobby steals from the business and all but ruins me in the process. That filled me with anger. Then you spend weeks hounding me for answers, which I deeply resented. Caleb dies. One of my best friends is devastated, and I am worried sick about her. My mentor is frantic about his wife's state of mind. You and I wind up in bed together, which makes me feel things I never imagined feeling. Bobby is hiding out in the Cayman Islands and uttering barely veiled threats, which scare me and infuriate me all at the same time.''

She regarded him with a bleak expression. ''Bottom line? All I feel right now is pressure. It's coming at me from every direction. I just want to shut it all out.''

''Including me?''

''Yes.'' She took a deep breath and met his gaze with troubled eyes. ''I'm sorry, but that's how I feel.''

Laid out like that, Rafe could understand her dismay and her confusion. ''No, I'm the one who's sorry. You have been through a lot. Maybe because you have always seemed so strong, I didn't take into account that this would be too much, even for you. What do you want me to do?''

''You asked me once before if I wanted you to go back to New York.'' Her eyes glistened with unshed tears. ''I do, Rafe. That's what I want.''

He swallowed hard, fighting the surprising hurt that came with her words. But he had asked, implying that he would do whatever she wanted, and she had given him an honest answer. He had to walk away. There was no other choice.

''Okay,'' he said quietly. ''I'll leave tomorrow.''

For an instant she looked taken aback by his ready agreement, maybe even a little disappointed. He had a feeling he was going to cling to the latter in the weeks to come.

''I'm sorry,'' she whispered, as the tears finally spilled over and ran unchecked down her cheeks.

''It's okay,'' he told her. ''I'm going now, but you're not getting rid of me for good. I'll be back.''

''When?''

He grinned at that. ''See, you miss me already, sweetheart. That should tell you something.''

What it told him was that he wasn't going to give Gina one minute more than necessary before coming back to claim her. She would have her space, her time to sort through the emotional turmoil and the tragedies of the past couple of months.

But he wasn't going to give her time to forget about him, to convince herself that what they had wasn't real. In fact, now that he knew without a doubt what he wanted, he was going to do everything in his power to make sure she understood that it was going to last a lifetime.

Gina started to miss Rafe almost the instant she watched his flight to New York take off. But even as tears stung her eyes, her friends closed ranks around her.

"He'll be back," Lauren predicted.

"When?" she asked wistfully, just as she had asked him the day before.

"When the time is right," Lauren assured her. "Something tells me Rafe O'Donnell is the kind of man who has a finely honed sense of timing. Besides that, the man is crazy in love with you."

Gina was startled by the assessment. "He is?"

"Well, of course he is," Emma said with a touch of exasperation. "Even I can see that."

Lauren chuckled. "Listen to Emma. She may be oblivious to the way Ford feels about her, but she can still recognize love when she spots it in anyone else."

"Oh, go suck an egg," Emma snapped.

"Is that what you say in a courtroom when you don't like what a judge has to say?" Lauren chided. "You must be held in contempt quite a lot."

"Sometimes I am, but it's worth it," Emma said loftily. "Now, let's go to the Heartbreak and have a beer. Tony's is closed tonight, so Gina doesn't have to work. I'm not due in court tomorrow. We can live it up. Maybe there will be some handsome men around who'll dance with us and make us forget everything else.''

Gina didn't hold out much hope that anything could take her mind off the fact that she had sent Rafe away, but she was willing to give it a try.

"I'm game,'' she said. "How about you, Lauren?''

"Count me in. I've always been a sucker for a handsome cowboy who can dance.''

"Since when?'' Gina asked. "You couldn't wait to get away from a whole town filled with cowboys.''

Lauren shrugged. "Times change. Are we going to talk this to death or do it?''

Gina cast one more look at the sky in the direction where she'd last seen Rafe's plane heading east. "Let's do it,'' she said finally.

Unfortunately, though, a couple of beers and the attention of a few men she'd known since childhood didn't do a thing to keep her from thinking about Rafe and the fact that she'd sent him away.

"He jumped at the chance to leave,'' she said despondently to Lauren. "Don't you think he was awfully eager to go?''

"No, what I think is that he was doing what you asked him to do, even though he didn't want to. Did you see how much paperwork he loaded into that plane? Boxes of it. That was a man who was settling in right here. If you'd asked, he probably would have left his firm in New York, opened an office in Winding River and stuck around indefinitely.''

"The town could use a really good lawyer,'' Emma said, her expression thoughtful. "If Rafe had been in practice here, instead of a seventy-year-old man who's still living in the Dark Ages, I wouldn't be running back and forth from Denver right now to handle Sue Ellen's case."

"I like having you coming back and forth," Gina protested. "I'm going to hate it when you go back to Denver full-time."

"Me, too," Karen agreed. "In fact, I think you should be the one opening a practice here."

"With Rafe as her partner," Lauren said, grinning. "Perfect. Everybody gets what they want."

"Rafe is with a huge firm in New York," Gina pointed out dryly. "I don't think he's into small-town law."

"Neither was Emma," Karen noted. "She hasn't said anything, but I heard she took on two other cases while she was here last week. I think that's very telling, don't you?"

"Whoa," Emma said. "Let's not leap to any conclusions here. Sue Ellen's case is a one-time thing, a tragic situation for someone we know. When it's over, that's that. I'll be back in Denver."

"What about the other cases?" Lauren asked.

"They were quickies," Emma insisted. "Nothing the least bit complicated. I wrote a will for someone and helped another person straighten out a billing error. They're both already over and done with."

"We'll see," Lauren said smugly. "I predict you'll decide to stay before the end of the trial. It's what Caitlyn wants. It's what your family wants. It is most definitely what Ford Hamilton wants."

Emma scowled. "Leave Ford out of this. He has nothing to do with any decision I make."

"I don't think he'll agree to be left out," Lauren teased. "Have you guys seen them together?"

"I've heard them," Karen said, grinning. "They argue. Morning, noon, night, it doesn't matter, they argue." She gave an exaggerated shiver. "All that untapped passion just waiting to cut loose."

"I refuse to listen to another word of this," Emma said with a huff. "I'm going home, where I will get a good night's sleep, untroubled by dreams of Ford Hamilton or any other man, for that matter."

"Give me a lift?" Gina asked. "I told Rafe I needed this time to think. I guess I'd better start doing it."

Lauren glanced at Karen. "I guess it's just you and me then. Can we stick around and listen to the music?"

"Sure," Karen agreed, though without much enthusiasm.

Gina gave a fierce hug to each of her friends. "Thanks for sticking by me tonight. Watching Rafe leave was harder than I'd expected it to be."

"All the more reason to get on the phone and tell him to come back, don't you think?" Lauren asked.

"Leave her alone," Emma advised. "She needs time to think."

"No," Lauren said adamantly. "What she needs is to listen to her heart for the first time in her life."

"Hey, you guys can stop talking about me as if I'm not here," Gina said, waving a protesting hand in front of their faces. "I don't know what I need or what I want or even what my heart is saying." She smiled to take the sting out of her words. "I'll keep you posted."

She got her first clue when she walked into her room at the hotel and saw the message light blinking. Sure that Rafe must have called, her heart thumped unsteadily. Filled with an unfamiliar sense of anticipation, she grabbed the phone and asked for the message.

"Deidre called," the desk clerk reported, dimming Gina's excitement. "She says it's urgent. Call her at the restaurant or at home, no matter what time it is."

"Thanks, Lucille," Gina told the woman. Now her heart was beating too hard for another reason entirely. She glanced at the clock, then dialed the restaurant's number. Deidre picked up at once. "Hi, it's Gina. What's going on?"

"Three of our biggest investors were in here earlier tonight demanding to see you or Bobby," she said without preamble. "I didn't know what to do, so I lied. I told them you were away on a family emergency and couldn't be reached and that Bobby was due back soon. They seemed to accept that."

Gina was surprised they'd bought it. "Are you sure they didn't know Bobby had taken off with the money?"

"Apparently not, or maybe they were on a fishing expedition. My hunch was that they'd heard rumors and came by to check them out, but they took my story at face value."

"Did they leave right away or cause trouble?"

"Neither. I invited them to stay for dinner. I made sure they had the best meal of their lives, a bottle of our best wine and great service. It didn't hurt that the place was packed. They left happy men. I still think you might want to call them, though, follow up on their visit, so to speak. I got their business cards."

"Give me the names," Gina said, taking them down. "I'll call first thing in the morning. Thanks again, Deidre. I honestly don't know what I'd do without you."

"Are you coming back soon?" Deidre asked wistfully. "I like running this place and I'm good at most of it, but dealing with this kind of thing gives me hives. I'm a wreck."

"But you did exactly the right thing," Gina said. "That fib you told was pretty close to the truth, and it got the job done."

"You didn't answer my question. Are you coming back soon?"

"Another couple of weeks," Gina said. "I promise."

By then Tony and Francesca should be back. With any luck Gina would have sorted through her own options and be ready to deal with the fallout, whichever way she went.

"Okay, I can hold the fort that long," Deidre said, sounding more optimistic. "By the way, I've managed to bring nearly half the bills up to date. If business stays like this for the rest of the fall, they should all be caught up by the time you get here. That'll just leave the payments to the investors for you to handle. And with the holidays coming and all the parties and catering, you should be in good shape."

"Business is that good?" Gina said, surprised and pleased. "We have catering jobs booked for the holidays?" There had been a trickle of requests for information before she'd left, but she'd expected word of their financial straits to make most people too skittish to book them for critical holiday entertaining.

"Business is great," Deidre said. "We have a big catering job for almost every night between Thanksgiving and New Year's. And Ronnie and I have been able to cut a few costs in the kitchen. Nothing to harm the quality of the food," she said hurriedly. "We're just cutting waste."

"Thank you again," Gina said with heartfelt sincerity, as an idea began to take shape in her head.

If her sous-chef and Deidre were doing such a great job of running Café Tuscany and the catering staff, maybe Gina could end up having it both ways. Maybe she could work out a partnership with them for the restaurant and the catering business, and divide her own time between Winding River and New York. It was definitely something to consider.

That just left Rafe. She would never have believed it a few weeks ago, but deciding what to do about him was a whole lot more complicated—and more important—than figuring out how to straighten out the mess that Bobby had left her in. She had a feeling that fate had brought him into her life for a reason, and she'd be a fool to let him get away.

No sooner had she said goodbye to Deidre than the phone rang again. She picked it up, still lost in thought. "Did you forget something?" she asked, assuming it was her manager calling back.

"Only you," Rafe said, his voice low and seductive. "I never should have left you behind."

Gina sighed and settled back against the pillows. Suddenly space didn't seem nearly as important as letting the sound of his voice wash over her. "Is that so?"

"Are you through thinking things over yet?"

She chuckled at the wistful note in his voice. Hearing that filled her with an amazing sense of satisfaction. "You've only been gone a few hours. I'm just getting started. Are you home now?"

"I'm in New York," he said. "Funny thing about that, though."

"What?"

"It doesn't feel half as much like home as that hotel room did, especially the last few nights."

"Oh, Rafe," she whispered. "You shouldn't say things like that."

"Why not? It's true."

"But it just makes it harder."

"Makes what harder?"

"Thinking."

He laughed. "I told you before, stop thinking so hard. This is something you have to decide from the gut."

"What is your gut telling you?" she asked curiously.

"That what I've found with you is too important to let slip away."

His words were oddly reassuring because they so closely echoed her own thoughts. He hadn't yet mentioned love. She had a feeling if he had she would have felt overwhelmed and even more pressured. These words simply hinted that what they had should be explored, tested...clung to until they knew exactly what it meant. She could live with that without panicking.

"Call me tomorrow?" she asked.

"Tomorrow and every day after," he said. "Sweet dreams, Gina."

If only, she thought. Something told her that without Rafe beside her, she'd be lucky to sleep at all, much less dream.

Chapter Fifteen

Rafe felt an overwhelming sense of relief when Charlie Flynn called to report that he had Bobby Rinaldi under surveillance in the Cayman Islands.

"He's living pretty quietly," Flynn said. "He's certainly not throwing his money around."

"What's your take on the guy?"

"Frankly, I was surprised. I expected a lot of flash and dazzle, a woman on each arm, especially after what you'd said about the way he took in your mother."

"And?"

"He's just an average guy. There are no women, though he hangs out at the hotel bar most evenings. If one comes on to him, he certainly flirts back, but he goes back to his room alone."

Rafe was as startled by that as Flynn. "That doesn't fit the image I had, either."

"What do you want me to do?" the investigator asked.

"Keep an eye on him. If the opportunity presents itself and you can do it without stirring up any suspicion, get to know him. See if you can figure out what his motive was in running out with all that cash."

"Will do," Flynn said. "I'll check in when I have something."

"Just don't lose track of him," Rafe warned.

"As if I would," the investigator said scathingly. "Not for what you're paying me. I don't shut my eyes for a second."

"I'm counting on that."

Rafe hung up, his expression thoughtful. Why would Bobby Rinaldi betray Gina, run off with all that cash and hide out in the Caymans? He'd left a reasonably clear trail, so Rafe doubted he was trying to drop out of sight to avoid paying heavy gambling debts. What else could it be? Was he in trouble with some married lover's husband? With the IRS? Rafe wondered if anyone at the restaurant might have a clue.

Knowing Gina would probably object, he didn't tell her his intentions. Instead, he dropped in at Café Tuscany just before opening the next day. From the instant he entered the soothing, classy foyer, he understood what Lydia had been saying all along about the place. It was a step above most flash-in-the-pan successes. Café Tuscany wasn't a trendy fluke. It was here to stay. Somehow he found that reassuring. It suggested that once she'd sorted through some things, Gina would be back. They could resume their relationship right here in New York, where they both belonged.

A slender, dark-haired woman wearing a simple, stylish black dress came toward him from the kitchen, a questioning expression on her face.

"We're not open for another half hour," she said with a warm smile.

"I know. You must be the famous Deidre that Gina has told me so much about."

Her expression faltered. "And you are?"

"Rafe O'Donnell."

"Ah," she said slowly. "The attorney for the investors."

Rafe tried not to let it matter that she'd heard of him only in his professional role, not as Gina's lover. Maybe that was for the best, since he was here to get answers.

"Some of them," he admitted. "If you have a minute, could we talk?"

She shook her head. "Without a subpoena, I have nothing to say to you."

"It won't take long," he promised, though he could see from her expression that time wasn't the issue. He was pretty sure he knew what was. He added, "It could help Gina."

That seemed to surprise her. "You want to help her?"

"Yes," he said with total sincerity.

She studied him intently, then nodded and led the way to a table. She gestured for him to sit.

"Would you like some coffee? A cappuccino?"

"Nothing, thanks."

She sat opposite him. "What do you want to know?"

"How well did you know Bobby Rinaldi?"

"Not intimately, if that's what you're suggesting," she said with a touch of indignation.

"I'm not suggesting anything improper," he soothed. "I'm just trying to get a picture of the guy. Why would he run off with all that money?"

"A woman," she said at once.

"But he's in the Cayman Islands all alone," Rafe said.

Her eyes widened. "You know where he is?"

"Yes."

"Does Gina know?"

He nodded. "Was Bobby a gambler?"

"No way," she said.

"A big spender?"

"Yes, but he had the money. His take out of here was pretty substantial."

Rafe was relatively certain that Gina had been taking very little out of the business. Why had Bobby gotten so much more? And why hadn't that shown up on the books he'd picked up from Deidre a couple of months back?

"More than Gina's salary?" he asked.

"I think so. I could look at the books. I've been paying bills while Gina's away."

It occurred to Rafe then that the books he'd been given had been for the restaurant's early years, not the current one. Perhaps quite a lot had changed in the months immediately before Bobby had disappeared.

"Let me take a look with you," he said, concluding there was no point in criticizing Deidre for not giving him the current financial records along with the others, even though the subpoena had been for everything.

He followed her into the office. She removed the latest record book from a file cabinet and opened it to the first of the year. Sure enough, Bobby's draw from the company was dramatically more than Gina's and higher than what he'd been taking out in past years. Had Gina known about that? Was it part of some deal they'd made? Maybe he was supposed to be paying the investors with the additional funds, though that would certainly be an unorthodox way of conducting business.

"Who wrote those checks? Gina or Bobby?" he asked Deidre.

"Until this mess, Bobby handled all of the financial details," she revealed. "I don't think Gina ever touched the checkbook, though she could sign checks if she needed to."

That must have been what Bobby had counted on, that she wouldn't even see the size of the checks he'd written to himself. He'd taken four careful years to establish a routine, then taken advantage of Gina after she'd been lulled into a false sense of complacency. Rafe's impression of the man, never very high, sank even lower.

"Thanks, Deidre," Rafe said when he'd jotted down a few notes. "One last thing. What was Bobby's relationship with Gina like?"

"He adored her," she said without hesitation. "In fact, I think he might have been half in love with her, though she wouldn't give him the time of day, not that way. He paraded women through here, but I always thought he did it because he was trying to get Gina to pay attention, not because he cared about any of them."

Deidre's assessment echoed in Rafe's head throughout the day and for the rest of the week. *He did it because he was trying to get Gina to pay attention. Pay attention. Pay attention.*

Dear God, was *that* what this had been about? Was this entire mess an attempt on Bobby Rinaldi's part to get Gina to look at him? It was a screwy idea, but once it occurred to Rafe, he couldn't seem to shake it. Goodness knows, *he* knew the power of her appeal. Why wouldn't Rinaldi, who was reputedly an expert on women? To a charming scoundrel used to getting any female he wanted, the one who proved immune was bound to be the most alluring.

There was only one way to find out if he'd hit on the answer, Rafe concluded. He needed to talk to Rinaldi face-to-face, to confront him with what he suspected and see how he reacted.

He called Charlie Flynn. "I'm coming down there. Make sure Rinaldi sits tight. I can't get away this week and possibly not next week. I'm due in court on a couple of cases, and I can't ask for postponements."

"He won't go anywhere," Flynn promised.

"Thanks." He hung up slowly. What if he was right? Did Gina suspect that Bobby might be in love with her? How would she feel if she knew? Was that the reason she was so hesitant to commit to Rafe, because she returned Bobby's unspoken feelings? Rafe really, really hated that idea, but he couldn't ignore it.

And until he knew a whole lot more than he knew right now, maybe it was best if he kept not only some physical distance between himself and Gina, but some emotional distance, as well. Losing her now wouldn't hurt any less than losing her later, but it might be just a little easier on his pride.

Rafe hadn't called for three weeks, not since the night he'd left town. Gina was beside herself trying to figure out what it meant. One minute she was furious with him, the next resigned, the next hurt.

"I don't get it," she said to Emma. "He was the one who was so anxious for us to see where things would go."

"He's probably just busy. He was away from New York for a long time. I'm sure he was swamped with work when he got back. I know the type. I *am* one," she admitted ruefully. "When I'm caught up in a case, I don't see anything else."

"I suppose," Gina said, but she didn't entirely buy it. And if this was the way a future with Rafe was going to play out, with him getting so caught up in work that he forgot all about her, did she want him in her life, anyway?

"If you want to know what's going on, call him," Emma advised. "You have his number."

"No. I'm the one who said I wanted space. I guess I ought to be grateful that he's giving it to me."

On top of Rafe's odd behavior, there was Bobby's. She hadn't heard a word from him, either. Nor had he sent a dime to pay off the restaurant's debts. She was half tempted to fly down to the Caymans and snatch back every penny he had stolen.

Of course, it was an idle threat. She couldn't go anywhere until Tony got back. He had called the week before and asked if she would mind if he and Francesca extended their stay in Italy.

"Who knows if we'll ever get back here again," he'd said. "We'd like to take advantage of our time here now, that is if you're sure you can stay on in Wyoming."

"I can stay," Gina said, praying that Deidre would understand the delay. "You and Francesca enjoy yourselves. How's her sister?"

"Much improved, thank goodness. Francesca is very relieved. In a few days her sister might even be well enough to go with us to Florence and Venice."

Gina had sighed. It sounded wonderful. She had loved her time in Italy. "Enjoy every minute of it," she told Tony. "And take lots of pictures."

"You are an angel, *cara mia*. And when I get home, there are things you and I must discuss."

"What things?"

"Not yet. Face-to-face," he insisted. "A few more weeks. No more. I don't want to take advantage of you."

"You could never take advantage of me," she told him. "I owe you way too much. If it's going to be longer than a week or so, though, would you mind if I closed for a few days so I can take a quick trip to New York? Everything's running smoothly at Café Tuscany right now, but I need to look in on Deidre before she starts feeling totally abandoned. Also, it might help me to decide a few things I've been thinking about.''

''Go, of course. Anything that will help you to clarify what you really want. Perhaps we are on the same wavelength,'' he said hopefully.

''Perhaps,'' she said, though she was not entirely certain what was on his mind. He'd been way too vague for her to interpret his intentions. ''I love you guys. I miss you. So do the customers.''

''I doubt that, when they have you,'' Tony scoffed. ''But it is nice of you to say.''

Ever since that conversation, she had been putting off the trip she had mentioned to Tony. With no word from Rafe and with Deidre still reporting that everything at Café Tuscany was under control, Gina lost the sense of urgency. In fact, the only place she felt truly needed was right here in Winding River. Tony needed her to stay. Karen seemed glad of her company. Her parents were delighted she was nearby, even if they thought it was absurd that she was wasting money on a hotel room when her room at home was empty. Maybe it *was* crazy, especially now that there was no longer any potential danger that she might be dragging them into her problems with Bobby.

In the end, though, purely by chance she happened across a small apartment with big windows, cozy nooks, comfortable furniture and a surprisingly spacious kitchen filled with light. It was tucked behind a house on Main Street, in what had once been a garage. She spotted the

For Rent sign while walking to Tony's one morning. The next day she stopped by to see it.

Now she stood in the middle of that kitchen and suddenly felt at peace. Without pausing to consider the ramifications, she pulled out her checkbook and turned to the owner.

"I'll take it," she told Mrs. Garwood.

"For how long? Are you home to stay?" her mother's friend asked. "I know that would please your mother."

Gina's hand faltered over the check. "I don't know," she admitted. "Is that a problem? Could we go month to month for now?"

"Normally I wouldn't agree to that," Mrs. Garwood said, then smiled. "But for your mother, I will take a chance that you'll decide you're back for good."

"Thank you," Gina said and wrote the check for a deposit and a month's rent.

"I'll leave you alone, then," Mrs. Garwood said. "If you need anything, just knock on the back door."

After she had gone, Gina turned slowly. The sun was streaming through the kitchen window. Funny, she thought, recalling Rafe's words a few weeks earlier. This place felt more like home already than the apartment she'd had in New York for years.

"He's right over there," Flynn told Rafe, pointing to an unremarkable-looking man sitting at the poolside bar, his expression glum as he sipped beer.

"That's Bobby Rinaldi?" Rafe asked, not even trying to hide his shock. He'd expected someone more handsome, but maybe Bobby's appeal wasn't obvious to a man.

It had taken Rafe almost a month to fit this trip into his schedule. The holidays were approaching. He wanted this settled so he could spend them with Gina. With any luck at all they could be engaged by New Year's.

"The one and only. Come on. I'll introduce you. We've had quite a few chats lately." Flynn hesitated. "Is he going to recognize your name?"

"Most likely."

"Want me to use an alias?"

Rafe grinned. "No, let's play it straight. What's the worst he can do?"

"Run," Flynn suggested.

"Maybe, but I'm sure you're faster, and between us we're not going to let him out of our sight until we get him back to New York."

"Whatever you say."

Flynn led the way across the deck, which was crowded with vacationers escaping the oncoming winter in the States. Soothed by bright sun and fancy rum drinks, many of them were half-asleep and oblivious to the sudden tension at the bar when Flynn made the introductions.

Once again surprising Rafe, Bobby looked more disappointed than fearful upon hearing his name. His expression lent credence to Rafe's theory that he was down here hoping that Gina would be the one to follow him.

"Expecting someone else?" Rafe inquired lightly. "Gina, perhaps?"

Bobby sighed heavily. "What did you do? Forbid her to come, so that you could be her knight in shining armor?"

"She doesn't know I'm here," Rafe said.

"Why not?"

"I wanted to clarify a few things before I filled her in." He gave Bobby a pointed look. "Or before you did that yourself."

"I'm not going back," Bobby said.

"There's a return ticket in your room that suggests otherwise," Flynn said.

Bobby frowned at him. "You searched my room?"

"Of course," Flynn said. "I wouldn't have been doing my job if I hadn't."

"You lousy, no-good creep," Bobby muttered, but without much venom. He seemed to have lost his enthusiasm for the game.

"Let's stay focused," Rafe suggested. "First question, why did you take that money?"

"Because I wanted it," Bobby said at once. "Why does anyone steal? Because they want something or they need it or just for the thrill of it."

"Really? You didn't do a very good job of covering your tracks. The payments to you were right on the books, but you counted on Gina not seeing them, at least not until after you'd taken off, right? So, I have a theory."

"Do share it," Bobby said sarcastically.

"You're in love with Gina," Rafe speculated, keeping his gaze fixed on Rinaldi's face. Sure enough there was a flicker of surprise in his eyes. He went on. "She wasn't interested in you. Now that the restaurant is doing so well, she doesn't even need you the way she once did. This was a way to get her to pay attention."

"If that was my plan, it certainly was a bust, wasn't it?" Bobby said, not quite admitting to it.

"Because she doesn't love you, except as a friend." Rafe regarded him with a surprising burst of compassion. "She does care about you, though. She was devastated by your betrayal. For weeks she tried to convince herself that you hadn't meant to ruin the business, to ruin her. She wouldn't lift a finger to help me nail you."

Bobby seemed surprised by that. "She wouldn't?"

"Not at first. One of the most amazing things about

Gina is her sense of loyalty. As time has passed, she has transferred that loyalty to the people you bilked out of money. Every single one of them will be paid back, no matter what it takes. She's committed to that, but she won't run to you to get the money. Her days of trusting you are over, Rinaldi. If your plan was to get her to need you, it backfired. She's found other people to count on."

"Like you," Bobby said with a sneer.

"I'm one of them, but there are lots more. It seems to me if you really care about her, though, you'll go back, return the money and keep her from having to struggle for months or even years to make it all right."

Bobby stared at him, first with defiance, then eventually in defeat. "What the hell?" he said at last. "I was getting sick of all this sunshine, anyway."

Rafe nodded. "Think of it this way. You'll be giving Gina the best Christmas present you could possibly give her, one she's not likely to forget."

Chapter Sixteen

Gina could no longer avoid her parents. They had been in the restaurant several times, asking questions, regarding her with undisguised worry. Each and every time, she had been busy enough to avoid responding to the interrogation. But on Thanksgiving Day, she knew that her time had run out.

"For once, you just sit there and let me cook," her mother commanded the minute Gina entered the kitchen. "I can certainly fix a turkey and stuffing. I've been doing it for years."

"I don't mind helping," Gina protested.

"I know that, but you need a break. You're working too hard trying to avoid making some tough decisions. At least that's the way it seems to your father and me. Are we right? Is this about Rafe or New York? Not that we aren't delighted that you're still here, but it's not like you to stay away from your business for so long, not when you spent so much time making it successful.''

"A lot's been happening," Gina said defensively. "First with Karen, then with Tony and Francesca. I couldn't abandon them."

"That's very noble, I'm sure, but I know you, my darling girl. Tony came back on Monday. Yet you're still here, still in that little apartment behind Nancy Garwood's house. That tells me that you're hiding from something."

Gina sighed. She had never been able to keep things from her mother, which was one reason she'd been steering clear of the house so much lately.

Gina toyed with a napkin. She folded it into an elaborate swan, then unfolded it and made a simple triangle more in keeping with her mother's table setting. The silence in the room deepened as her mother stirred the pots on the stove and waited for a reply to her question. Gina recognized that she wasn't going to be able to avoid giving an answer.

"You know about the problem with the business," she said. "That's how Rafe and I met. He thought I had something to do with Bobby stealing that money. He distrusted me."

"But you fell for him, anyway," her mother said. "And he for you. So you got past the initial distrust and resentment."

Gina nodded and reached for a carrot stick just to have something to hold.

"Then you're not hiding from Rafe?"

"Actually I am, in a way." She sighed heavily. "It's complicated."

"Because you've fallen in love with him," her mother concluded. "And that scares you."

The carrot stick snapped in half. Gina stared at it in

surprise, then looked at her mother with even greater shock. "You can see that?"

Her mother grinned. "Darling, you never were any good at hiding your emotions. Even your father figured this part out. What we didn't understand was why you didn't just admit it. It's obvious he cares about you, too. Whatever complications there were at the beginning will resolve themselves in time."

"I thought so, too, for a while, but he hasn't been in touch lately. And now there's another wrinkle. It just came up this week when Tony got back."

"What's that?"

"Tony asked me to go into partnership with him." She took a deep breath, knowing that her parents were going to be delighted by the news, though they would never try to influence her decision. "He and Francesca want to spend more time in Italy. He says eventually the business would be mine, if I want to stay here."

Just as she'd expected, her mother was wise enough not to reveal her reaction. Instead, she asked, "How do you feel about that?"

Gina permitted herself a slight grin. "I really, really want to do it. Despite all of the chaos the past few months, I've loved being here. Until I came back I hadn't realized how much I missed you guys and my friends and even Winding River. I really don't want to live in New York anymore."

"Which brings us back to Rafe," her mother guessed.

"Exactly."

"There's only one way to figure out what to do," she told Gina. "You have to go to New York, settle things with Rafe and with Café Tuscany, then make a final decision. You can't make such an important decision in a vacuum, certainly not from here, when everything involved is across the country.''

"You're absolutely right," Gina said, reaching the same conclusion. "That is exactly what I have to do. If I can get a flight, I'll go in the morning."

Unfortunately, because of the holiday, she couldn't get a flight until the middle of the following week. When she called Rafe's office from the airport, they told her he was out of town on business and not expected back for a day or two.

"Is this Lydia?" Gina asked.

"Yes."

"This is Gina Petrillo. When he gets back, will you tell him I'm in New York and that I'd like to see him?"

"You're back? That's fantastic. I know you'll be the first person he wants to see when he gets back. I'll tell him," she said. "I'm glad you're here."

Gina wasn't quite sure what to make of that. Since the next stop on her agenda was Café Tuscany, she put off considering Lydia's words until later and took a cab straight from the airport to the restaurant.

When she walked through the front door, waves of pride and nostalgia washed over her. The restaurant was every bit as elegant and tasteful as she'd remembered. She had accomplished that, she and Bobby.

As she stood there basking in the good memories, Deidre stepped out of the kitchen and caught sight of her. Her eyes lit with delight. "You're back," she said, striding across the room to hug Gina. "I am so glad to see you. We have really missed you around here."

"It doesn't look like it. The place looks terrific."

Deidre waved off the compliment. "The cleaning crew keeps it spotless. Are you here to stay?"

"We need to talk about that," Gina said. "Can you come into the office? Is Ronnie here?"

"He's in the kitchen. Shall I get him?"

"Do that and bring some cappuccino with you," Gina suggested. "I need a jolt of caffeine."

When the two of them were settled into the chairs opposite her desk in the cramped office, she announced, "I've been doing a lot of thinking while I've been away."

Deidre's face fell. "You're going to close it down, aren't you? You're going to stay in Wyoming and close this place down. I knew it when you didn't come back right away. That Tony guy you were always talking about made you an offer too good to refuse."

"Whoa!" Gina said, chuckling at the rush of words. "You're only half-right. I am considering the possibility of staying in Wyoming."

Ronnie Carson, a quiet young man with a good head on his shoulders, as well as tremendous potential as a chef, studied her intently before he spoke. "But you have a plan for this place, don't you? You're not just going to shut the door and walk away."

"No, but whether or not it is feasible depends on the two of you and what you want."

As Deidre and Ronnie exchanged a look, Gina thought she caught a glimpse of something more than colleagues awaiting word on their fate. She had a feeling they had discovered each other while she was away. There was a distinct stirring of romance in the air. Maybe they'd wind up like Tony and Francesca, bound not only by love, but by working together at something they loved.

"Okay, here's the deal," she said. "Since you have managed to not only keep this place afloat under extremely daunting conditions, but to make it thrive, it occurred to me that you might be interested in taking over for me permanently.''

''You mean we'd go on running it?'' Deidre asked cautiously, her expression brightening ever so slightly.

''And eventually buy it from me,'' Gina said. ''I'm in no rush about this. I don't need the money for what I want to do in Wyoming, at least not right away. We could work out a price and an arrangement that would give you time to get your feet on the ground financially. That could take a while because the first thing we'd need to do is get all of the old investors paid off. But I'd say in four or five years this would be yours, if you want it. Are you interested?''

''Ohmigosh,'' Deidre whispered, her gaze on Ronnie. ''What do you think? Can we do it?''

He met her gaze, eyes shining, his expression serious. ''Of course we can. If it's what you want. Is it?''

She reached for his hand. ''Yes. Absolutely. And you?''

A half smile tugged at his lips. ''It's the answer to a prayer.''

Gina suddenly felt completely serene. She was making the right decision. She didn't have a single doubt about it. Not only was she making Ronnie and Deidre deliriously happy, but she was getting what she wanted, as well. Everybody would win.

The only potential blot on her happiness was Rafe's reaction. Maybe she should have consulted him first, but this was her business, her decision. Her relief at finally having made it was astonishing. She felt as if a two-ton weight had been lifted off her shoulders.

Now all she had to do was wrap up her personal affairs and wait for Rafe. It sounded so simple, but in her heart she knew there was going to be nothing simple about telling him that she intended to move a couple of thousand miles away for good.

Over the next twenty-four hours, Gina put all of her business affairs in order. She contacted each and every vendor to explain about the forthcoming changes and to assure them that their accounts would be settled and that she hoped they would continue to do business with Deidre and Ronnie. Most of them had such high praise for the two that she was certain they were going to succeed.

She also called all of the investors with a similar message, reassuring them that despite recent difficulties their investment was not only safe but would soon be extremely profitable. Satisfied that she was leaving town with her good name intact—at least as solid as it could be under the circumstances—she left her office for what she anticipated to be the last time and went back to her apartment to finish packing.

When the doorbell rang, to her total astonishment she found not just Rafe on her doorstep, but Bobby, as well.

"I tracked down a friend of yours," Rafe said unnecessarily. "He has something he wants to say to you before we go off to talk to the D.A. about the charges he's facing."

Bobby didn't look as if he were in a particularly talkative mood, but Rafe towered over him, and his grim expression never wavered.

"I'm sorry," Bobby said finally. "This was all a huge mistake."

"A mistake!"

He nodded. "I got some crazy idea in my head that you would turn to me if the business were in trouble."

Gina stared at him incredulously. "Why would you do something like that?"

Bobby remained mute, until Rafe scowled at him. "Tell her, Rinaldi. All of it. She deserves to know why you turned her life upside down."

"Because I'm in love with you," Bobby said in a voice that was little more than a whisper. "I have been since we met. But the only time you even looked at me was when we were pulling the business together. I wanted that back again."

She tried to make sense of it, but she couldn't. "You had to know I would blame you, not turn to you."

"Like I said, I wasn't thinking very clearly. I was sitting down in the Caymans waiting for you to come down and give me hell. It would have been better than the indifference I usually felt from you. I dated all those women, paraded them under your nose, and nothing. You didn't care."

"Oh, Bobby," she whispered. She couldn't make herself regret how this was turning out for her, but she was brokenhearted over the damage he had done not only to the business, but to the rest of his life. She looked at Rafe. "What happens now?"

"We have an appointment at the D.A.'s office. A lot depends on how much of the money he still has and pays back."

"It's all there," Bobby assured her. "Every penny."

"Then they should go easy on him," Rafe promised. He glanced at the packing boxes and her luggage. "Running again, Gina?"

"No," she said with certainty. "Not running away. Going home. When you get back I'll explain."

He nodded. "I'll be counting on it."

As he and Bobby went out the door, Bobby turned back. "I really am sorry. I never meant for you to be left holding the bag. I really didn't."

"I know," she said quietly, and to her surprise, she really did believe that.

Rafe had had a nasty moment when he'd seen the state of Gina's apartment. Even before she'd explained, he had known that she intended to go straight back to Wyoming. What he didn't know was what that meant for the two of them. He had some ideas of his own, decisions he'd made over the past few weeks, but he wasn't so sure they meshed with her plans.

When he returned to her apartment, he found her dressed in some sort of velvety robe that covered her from her shoulders to her feet. Oddly enough, it was the sexiest thing he'd ever seen her wear.

Despite the chaos in the apartment, she had a fire blazing on the gas logs. The lights were turned down low, and she'd opened a bottle of extremely expensive wine.

"Interesting," he said as he looked around. "If I didn't know better, I'd say you were out to seduce me." A smile came and went. "Again."

"What if I am?"

"I'd have to ask why."

"Because I want you to know exactly what I'm feeling, exactly what I want," she said at once.

"Sex?"

She grinned. "That, too."

"What else?"

"You," she said evenly. "I want you to come back to Wyoming with me. I know it's a lot to ask, that your law practice is here, but you were happy there, once you got used to it, anyway, and I think you love me and—"

"Yes," he said, interrupting her.

Her eyes widened. "What?"

He grinned. "If that was a proposal, the answer is yes."

"That easy?"

"You wanted me to be difficult?"

"Well, I did have all these very persuasive arguments I was hoping to use," she said, moving into his arms.

He lowered his head to capture her mouth. Only after she had been thoroughly kissed, did he take a step back. "By all means," he teased, "persuade me, but I've got to tell you, I'm an easy mark where you're concerned. I have been since the beginning."

"Not since the beginning," she argued.

"Definitely the beginning," he insisted. "In fact, I've been considering a partnership of sorts with you for some time now."

"My experience with partnerships hasn't been all that great," she reminded him. "I told Tony I'd come back and work with him. I've known him my whole life. He would never betray me."

"Maybe not, but this thing with you and me would be a very personal partnership," Rafe pointed out. "No comparison."

"Can I trust you not to run out on me?"

"Absolutely."

"What are the terms? I want to know exactly what I'm getting into."

"Love, honor and cherish. Now and forever. The usual."

It sounded like a pretty decent deal. "Just one more thing. I intend to work for Tony. Eventually I'll take over. If the place is swamped, are you going to help cook?"

"Only if the chef rewards me later."

Gina held out her hand. "It's a deal."

But—typical lawyer—Rafe wasn't satisfied until they'd sealed it with a lot more than a handshake.

Epilogue

There had never been a doubt in the world about where their wedding reception was going to be held. Tony and Francesca started planning it the day Gina and Rafe shared the news that they were getting married. Now that the day had arrived, however, Tony had barred Gina from the kitchen.

"I will do this, *cara mia.* You are not to worry."

"But I could help," Gina protested uselessly. "Besides, I'm the bride. Shouldn't I have some say over what the cake looks like, at least?"

Tony regarded her with exaggerated indignation. "Do you not think that my Francesca knows what will please you?"

"Of course, but—"

"Go," Tony ordered. "The wedding is in an hour. You must be beautiful."

"Okay, okay," she said, though she didn't think an

hour was going to make much difference. The summer heat had already frizzed her hair, and it would melt her makeup the moment it was applied.

The instant she stepped outside the restaurant, she was surrounded by the Calamity Janes. "Francesca called you, didn't she?"

"She did," Emma said. "She said you were getting in her way."

"I wasn't in her way. Tony wouldn't even let me near the kitchen."

"This is one meal you are not going to cook yourself," Karen insisted. "Besides, as bridesmaids it is our duty to make sure you're dressed and at the church on time. You don't want to make us look bad, do you?"

Cassie was amazingly quiet as she studied Gina. "Prewedding jitters?" she asked eventually.

Gina gulped and nodded. "How did you know?"

Cassie and Karen exchanged knowing looks. "Been there, done that," they said in unison.

"Trust us, though, you are going to be deliriously happy. Rafe will see to it."

Gina smiled at last. "He already has."

"Well then," Emma said briskly. "There's nothing to worry about, is there? Let's get this show on the road. I have my list right here. If we follow it, we'll stay right on schedule."

Gina chuckled. "Wait till it's your turn," she warned Emma. "We are going to show you no mercy."

"I predict this fall," Lauren said.

"Definitely before Christmas," Karen said.

"Oh—" Emma began.

"Go suck an egg," they all chimed in. "You're not convincing anymore, Emma, so give it up," Lauren added. "You and Ford are next."

Gina looked around at her best friends and felt tears begin to well up in her eyes. She loved these women, and thanks to Bobby's treachery and Rafe's understanding, she had them back in her life. The Calamity Janes were a gift worth treasuring. She'd never lose sight of that again.

"Oh, no, she's about to start blubbering," Cassie noted. "Stop that, right this second. You can't get married with your eyes all red and puffy."

"Rafe won't care," she said with a sniff.

"Maybe not, but you will when you have to look at the wedding pictures in the years to come," Lauren added, giving her a hug. "Trust me on this. If there's one thing I know about it's how a bad picture can turn up years later to bite you in the butt."

They got her to the church and into her gown with five minutes to spare. She spent those minutes with her parents.

"Thank you," she said, hugging them fiercely.

"For what? The wedding? It was our pleasure," her mother said. "We've dreamed of this day for a long time."

"Not just that," Gina told them, holding her father's hand tightly. "For letting me go all those years ago and for welcoming me back now."

"Just give us some grandbabies and you will have paid us back in full," her mother said. Her father scowled. "Don't rush the girl, Jane. She hasn't even said 'I do' yet."

"That's okay," she told her father. "I think mother and Rafe are on the same page on that one. For a man who claimed to know nothing about relationships or family, he's adapting to the concept pretty quickly."

"How does that mother of his feel about being a

grandma?'' her father asked. ''I can't imagine she's happy about it. I've never seen a woman so determined to shave twenty years off her age.''

Gina grinned at the assessment. It was true. Rafe's mother worked astonishingly hard at being youthful. Grandchildren were going to rattle her.

''She'll adapt,'' Gina's mother said. ''And if she doesn't, I'll get those precious grandbabies all to myself.''

There was a knock on the door just then. ''I think they're ready for us,'' Cassie called out. ''And Rafe is prowling around the front of the church looking impatient.''

Gina opened the door. ''Then by all means, let's not keep the man waiting.''

Rafe had worn dozens of tuxedos in his time, but he was fairly certain this one was going to choke him to death. He ran his finger under the shirt collar.

''Stop fidgeting,'' his mother mouthed from the front pew.

The admonition made him grin despite himself. How many times had he heard that as a boy? A million, probably. It was good to know that some things never changed.

At last the music began, and his gaze flew to the back of the church. The procession seemed endless. First Cassie, Lauren, Karen and his own sister as the bridesmaids. Then Emma, looking softer and more feminine than he'd ever seen her, as Gina's maid of honor. Finally Caitlyn as the flower girl, happily scattering rose petals along the aisle as she grinned at Rafe.

There was a pause in the music, and Rafe's breath caught in his throat. Gina appeared on her father's arm, and his throat went dry. How had he ever gotten so lucky? Her dress was simple, but she looked like a million bucks in it. He grinned at the thought. That was exactly the price tag that had been put on Café Tuscany a few weeks ago, when the paperwork for Gina's deal with Deidre and Ronnie was being drawn up. All three of them had stared at the bankers in disbelief. Gina had insisted that the deal be for less than half of that.

"They've paid the difference a thousand times over," she had told the bankers. "It's because of them that it's worth so much now."

To Rafe's amusement she had gotten her way and the deal had been struck. Now there was nothing left to tie them to New York. They were in Winding River to stay.

"I love you," he whispered when Gina reached his side.

"You'd better," she whispered back, but her eyes were filled with laughter.

When the time came for the vows they had written for themselves, Rafe shocked the crowd with his first words. He could hear the gasps as he began by saying, "From the moment I met you, I knew you were a thief."

The only person who wasn't the least bit startled was Gina. She watched him solemnly with love in her eyes.

"You stole my heart," he said quietly, drawing a relieved sigh from the onlookers and the beginnings of a smile from Gina. "Even when I struggled to get it back, you held on and taught me what it means to share love and friendship. You taught me about loyalty and commitment. Today I give you my heart willingly, because I know you'll keep it safe forever."

There were tears shining in her eyes when he finished. She brushed at them impatiently as she began her own vows. "I know the value of what you are giving me, because I know how difficult it was for you to overcome all of the doubts you had about me at the beginning. It's a funny thing about distrust. It can destroy a relationship or it can make it stronger. I think ours is stronger because of the way it began. I will spend a lifetime proving to you that I deserve your trust and giving you everything that my heart has to share—my family, my friends, my town, and most of all, my love.''

When the priest pronounced them man and wife and blessed them, Gina held her face up for his kiss. Rafe covered her mouth with his own, and once again he was back at the fairgrounds on a hot, steamy afternoon, tasting her lips for the very first time, unable to stop, savoring every single second of the kiss.

The congregation erupted into laughter and applause when he finally released her. Gina grinned.

''I guess we're destined to giving them something to talk about,'' she said.

He winked. ''It certainly works for me. How about you?''

''Any time. Any place.''

''Forever?''

She stood on tiptoe and kissed him again, another slow, melting kiss that rocked him to his core.

''Definitely forever,'' she said.

* * * * *

*And now, turn the page
for a sneak preview of*

THE CALAMITY JANES,

*book four in Sherryl Woods's
exciting new miniseries,*
THE CALAMITY JANES,
*on sale in October 2001
from Silhouette Single Title*

Chapter One

Ford hadn't intended to go anywhere near the Winding River High School class reunion. He'd assigned Teddy Taylor to cover it and had given him a camera to take along. Teddy had been ecstatic.

"Be sure you get a few shots of Lauren Winters," he reminded the teenager. "Everyone's going to want to see the big celebrity deigning to mingle with the small-town folks."

Ford's sarcasm was unmistakable, even to Teddy. The boy frowned. "I don't think Lauren's like that. Uncle Ryan says she's great. She was the smartest kid in the class. He says she was real serious back then. Nobody expected her to wind up an actress."

"Whatever," Ford said, dismissing the ardent defense. "Just get lots of pictures. You probably know better than I do who's important."

"I hope so. I got a list from Uncle Ryan. He knows

everybody. There's a lady named Gina who has one of the hottest restaurants in New York—''

"Gina Petrillo?" Ford asked, startled. "Owns a place called Café Tuscany?"

Teddy glanced at his notes, then nodded. "Yeah, that's it. You've heard of it?"

"I've eaten there," he said. The editors of a New York paper had taken him there when they'd been courting him, trying to steal him away from an investigative team in Chicago. He'd been impressed by the food and the ambience, if not by the New Yorkers' pitch. The owner's name had stuck with him, though he'd only caught a glimpse of her as she rushed from the kitchen to greet favored guests. Discovering that Gina Petrillo came from Winding River was a surprise.

"And there's someone named Emma, who's some kind of courtroom barracuda in Denver now," Teddy continued. "And Cole Davis, the big computer-programming genius—well, he wasn't in the class, but his girlfriend was. Uncle Ryan says he'll probably be there even though he's a couple of years older."

Ford had been even more startled by the complete litany of success stories. Even though he'd come from a small town himself, he'd always felt that the odds of success were stacked against him. To find so many high achievers coming out of one small class in Winding River—okay, two classes, if Cole Davis had been a year or two ahead of the others—was intriguing.

The more he'd thought about it, the more convinced he'd become that there was a story there. Who or what had motivated these four people to work so hard? Was it a teacher? A parent? A community-wide commitment to education? Their stories could well provide motivation for the current crop of students.

Because of his fascination with the idea, Ford had bought a ticket to the Saturday-night dance. He had his tape recorder in his pocket, but for the moment he was content to stand on the fringes of the party and watch the dancing.

It was early yet. There was plenty of time for tracking down the class celebrities. Not that he expected to have any difficulty identifying them. The others would probably be fawning all over them, with the possible exception of the attorney. They might be giving her a wide berth. In his experience, most sensible people were wary of lawyers.

"Young man, why aren't you dancing?" Geraldine Hawkins demanded.

Ford glanced down into twinkling blue eyes framed by gray bangs. The veteran English teacher was sixty-five and barely five feet tall. Yet, according to Ron Haggerty, she could intimidate a six-five two-hundred and forty-pound linebacker. She'd been one of the first people Ford had met, the introduction preceded by an admonition not to underestimate her. Mrs. Hawkins, despite her diminutive size, was a well-respected powerhouse in town. A decade ago, she had been mayor twice, but now she claimed she no longer had time for that "nonsense."

She stood before him now with increasing impatience. "Well, young man?"

"Two left feet," Ford told her.

"I don't believe that for a minute." She gestured across the room to five women sitting at a table with one man. One of those women was unmistakably the gorgeous Lauren Winters. Another he recognized as Gina Petrillo. "Now go on over there and ask someone to dance. Nobody should be a wallflower at their own class reunion, especially not when there's a handsome, available man in the room.''

Ford grinned at her. ''I'd rather dance with you, Mrs. Hawkins. How about it? Care to take a spin around the floor with me?''

Color flamed in her cheeks, but she demurely held out her hand. ''Why, I don't mind if I do. Just stay off of my toes, young man. I have corns.''

He laughed at that. ''I'll do my best, but I'm not making any promises.''

He swept her into his arms and waltzed her gracefully around the floor. When the music ended, she scolded, ''Young man, you fibbed to me. You know perfectly well how to dance.''

''You inspired me, Mrs. Hawkins,'' he insisted.

''Nonsense. Now go ask someone your own age to dance.''

''Anyone in particular?''

She glanced over at the same group of women. One of them was clutching a cell phone to her ear and nodding, her expression intense. She was beautiful in an uptight, regal way, Ford mused.

''I'd recommend Emma Rogers,'' Mrs. Hawkins said. ''The one on the phone. She needs a distraction. Whoever invented cell phones ought to be shot, but since it's too late for that, we can only try to get them away from the people who are addicted to them.''

''Emma Rogers?'' Ford repeated, recalling his conversation with Teddy. ''She's an attorney?''

''A fine one, from what I've heard. Works too hard, though. I've heard that, as well. Just look at her. Here she is at a dance with all of her old friends and she's on the phone. I guarantee you that it's a business call.''

Even as they stared at her, Emma reluctantly handed

the phone to Lauren, who dialed, spoke to someone, then hung up, her expression triumphant. When Emma reached for the phone, Lauren held it away from her.

"Good for Lauren," Mrs. Hawkins said approvingly. "Now it's up to you. Ask her to dance. If ever there was a young woman in need of some fun, it's our Emma."

Ford sensed that the teacher was not going to give up until he was back out on the dance floor, preferably with the workaholic attorney. Since he'd intended to seek Emma out anyway, he nodded. "You win. But if I step all over her toes and she sues me, I'm holding you responsible."

"I'm not concerned," the English teacher said with a blithe expression.

Ford crossed the high school gym. By the time he reached the table, Emma was sitting all alone, her expression glum.

"I've been commanded to dance with you," Ford told her.

She gazed up at him, her expression startled. "Commanded? Now there's a gracious invitation, if ever I heard one."

"Mrs. Hawkins," he said, nodding in the teacher's direction.

To his surprise, a smile spread across Emma's face, softening the harsh lines of her mouth and putting a sparkle into her eyes. "She does have a way of getting what she wants, doesn't she? She actually managed to nudge me into reading Shakespeare. I hated it, but she never once let up. Eventually I began to like it."

"She must not have had to nudge too hard," Ford said. "From what I hear, you were a terrific student. I'm Ford Hamilton, by the way."

Her expression cooled considerably. "Ah," she said, "the new owner of the paper. I've heard about you."

"Nothing too damning, I hope."

"So far no, but then you've only been here a few weeks. I'm sure you haven't done your worst yet." She stood up. "Thanks for asking me to dance, but I have some old friends I need to see."

She brushed past him and headed straight for the hall-way. Ford stared after her, wondering what he'd said to offend her. Or was it nothing more than the fact that he owned the paper?

"Ms. Rogers?" he called after her.

She hesitated but didn't turn around. Refusing to talk to her back, he walked over and stepped in front of her.

"When you have a few minutes, I'd like to speak with you," he said.

Her expression remained cool. "About?"

"What or who motivated you when you were at Winding River High. I'm hoping to talk to all of the major success stories from your class. I think there might be some lessons in what drove you to succeed."

Her gaze narrowed. "What's your measure of success, Mr. Hamilton? Fame? Money?"

"Both, I suppose."

"Then we have nothing to talk about. You see, the people I view as successful from our class are the ones who are doing what they love to do, who are happy with their lives. For instance, my friend Karen. She's not famous and she probably has very little savings. But she's working a ranch she loves with a man she adores. That's success, Mr. Hamilton. Not what *I* do."

Before he could respond, there was a scuffle of some kind across the gym. A man who looked as if he was probably drunk was tugging on the arm of a woman, while another man looked as if he might intervene. Only after a subtle nod from the woman did the second man back away with a shrug. Finally he turned and left the room.

Beside Ford, Emma tensed. He glanced down and saw genuine worry on her face. "You know them?"

"Of course. Everyone in Winding River knows everyone else. Sue Ellen was in my class. Donny was a year older. They were high school sweethearts."

"They don't look so happy now," Ford observed. "Would they qualify as one of your success stories?"

"I really couldn't say. I haven't kept up," Emma replied frostily. "Look, Mr. Hamilton, I wish you luck with the paper—I really do. Winding River needs a good newspaper. But I'm not interested in being interviewed."

"Not even for the sake of inspiring a student?"

"Not even for that," she said firmly. "Now you really will have to excuse me."

"Has the media given you a tough time, Ms. Rogers?" he asked, halting her in her tracks. "Is that why you won't take five minutes out of your busy schedule to talk to a reporter from your hometown paper?"

Eyes flashing, she faced him. "Why I don't care to talk to you is my business. The bottom line is that I won't. Good night, Mr. Hamilton."

This time when she walked away, Ford let her go. He'd run across her type before. She wouldn't be above using the media if it served her purposes, but the rest of the time she treated each and every journalist with disdain. He hadn't expected to run across that kind of attitude in Winding River, but, of course, Emma Rogers lived in Denver now. Whatever bee she had in her bonnet about reporters came from a bad experience there. He'd bet his tape recorder on that.

He should let it pass. What did it matter if she didn't

want to talk to him? He had other prospects for his story. But the competitive part of him that hated being beat out of any potential scoop rebelled. First thing in the morning, he'd go on the Internet and do a search of the archives of the Denver papers. If Emma Rogers was as high profile as everyone said, there were bound to be mentions. They would give him some insight into what made the woman tick.

Once he knew that…well, it remained to be seen what he would do with the information.

If you enjoyed what you just read,
then we've got an offer you can't resist!

Take 2 bestselling
love stories FREE!
Plus get a FREE surprise gift!

Clip this page and mail it to Silhouette Reader Service™

IN U.S.A.
3010 Walden Ave.
P.O. Box 1867
Buffalo, N.Y. 14240-1867

IN CANADA
P.O. Box 609
Fort Erie, Ontario
L2A 5X3

YES! Please send me 2 free Silhouette Special Edition® novels and my free surprise gift. After receiving them, if I don't wish to receive anymore, I can return the shipping statement marked cancel. If I don't cancel, I will receive 6 brand-new novels every month, before they're available in stores! In the U.S.A., bill me at the bargain price of $3.80 plus 25¢ shipping and handling per book and applicable sales tax, if any*. In Canada, bill me at the bargain price of $4.21 plus 25¢ shipping and handling per book and applicable taxes**. That's the complete price and a savings of at least 10% off the cover prices—what a great deal! I understand that accepting the 2 free books and gift places me under no obligation ever to buy any books. I can always return a shipment and cancel at any time. Even if I never buy another book from Silhouette, the 2 free books and gift are mine to keep forever.

235 SEN DFNN
335 SEN DFNP

Name	(PLEASE PRINT)	
Address	Apt.#	
City	State/Prov.	Zip/Postal Code

* Terms and prices subject to change without notice. Sales tax applicable in N.Y.
** Canadian residents will be charged applicable provincial taxes and GST.
  All orders subject to approval. Offer limited to one per household and not valid to
  current Silhouette Special Edition® subscribers.
  ® are registered trademarks of Harlequin Enterprises Limited.

SPED01 ©1998 Harlequin Enterprises Limited

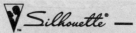

**SILHOUETTE®
MAKES YOU
A STAR!**

Feel like a star with Silhouette.

We will fly you and a guest to New York City for an exciting weekend stay at a glamorous 5-star hotel. Experience a refreshing day at one of New York's trendiest spas and have your photo taken by a professional. Plus, receive $1,000 U.S. spending money!

Flowers...long walks...dinner for two... how does Silhouette Books make romance come alive for you?

Send us a script, with 500 words or less, along with visuals (only drawings, magazine cutouts or photographs or combination thereof). Show us how Silhouette Makes Your Love Come Alive. Be creative and have fun. No purchase necessary. All entries must be clearly marked with your name, address and telephone number. All entries will become property of Silhouette and are not returnable. **Contest closes September 28, 2001.**

Please send your entry to: **Silhouette Makes You a Star!**

In U.S.A.	In Canada
P.O. Box 9069	P.O. Box 637
Buffalo, NY, 14269-9069	Fort Erie, ON, L2A 5X3

Look for contest details on the next page, by visiting www.eHarlequin.com or request a copy by sending a self-addressed envelope to the applicable address above. Contest open to Canadian and U.S. residents who are 18 or over. Void where prohibited.

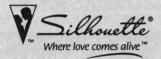

Silhouette®
Where love comes alive™

Our lucky winner's photo will appear in a Silhouette ad. Join the fun!

SRMYAS1

HARLEQUIN "SILHOUETTE MAKES YOU A STAR!" CONTEST 1308
OFFICIAL RULES
NO PURCHASE NECESSARY TO ENTER

1. To enter, follow directions published in the offer to which you are responding. Contest begins June 1, 2001, and ends on September 28, 2001. Entries must be postmarked by September 28, 2001, and received by October 5, 2001. Enter by hand-printing (or typing) on an 8 ½" x 11" piece of paper your name, address (including zip code), contest number/name and attaching a script containing 500 words or less, along with drawings, photographs or magazine cutouts, or combinations thereof (i.e., collage) on no larger than 9" x 12" piece of paper, describing how the Silhouette books make romance come alive for you. Mail via first-class mail to: Harlequin "Silhouette Makes You a Star!" Contest 1308, (in the U.S.) P.O. Box 9069, Buffalo, NY 14269-9069, (in Canada) P.O. Box 637, Fort Erie, Ontario, Canada L2A 5X3. Limit one entry per person, household or organization.

2. Contests will be judged by a panel of members of the Harlequin editorial, marketing and public relations staff. Fifty percent of criteria will be judged against script and fifty percent will be judged against drawing, photographs and/or magazine cutouts. Judging criteria will be based on the following:

   - Sincerity—25%
   - Originality and Creativity—50%
   - Emotionally Compelling—25%

   In the event of a tie, duplicate prizes will be awarded. Decisions of the judges are final.

3. All entries become the property of Torstar Corp. and may be used for future promotional purposes. Entries will not be returned. No responsibility is assumed for lost, late, illegible, incomplete, inaccurate, nondelivered or misdirected mail.

4. Contest open only to residents of the U.S. (except Puerto Rico) and Canada who are 18 years of age or older, and is void wherever prohibited by law; all applicable laws and regulations apply. Any litigation within the Province of Quebec respecting the conduct or organization of a publicity contest may be submitted to the Régie des alcools, des courses et des jeux for a ruling. Any litigation respecting the awarding of a prize may be submitted to the Régie des alcools, des courses et des jeux only for the purpose of helping the parties reach a settlement. Employees and immediate family members of Torstar Corp. and D. L. Blair, Inc., their affiliates, subsidiaries and all other agencies, entities and persons connected with the use, marketing or conduct of this contest are not eligible to enter. Taxes on prizes are the sole responsibility of the winner. Acceptance of any prize offered constitutes permission to use winner's name, photograph or other likeness for the purposes of advertising, trade and promotion on behalf of Torstar Corp., its affiliates and subsidiaries without further compensation to the winner, unless prohibited by law.

5. Winner will be determined no later than November 30, 2001, and will be notified by mail. Winner will be required to sign and return an Affidavit of Eligibility/Release of Liability/Publicity Release form within 15 days after winner notification. Noncompliance within that time period may result in disqualification and an alternative winner may be selected. All travelers must execute a Release of Liability prior to ticketing and must possess required travel documents (e.g., passport, photo ID) where applicable. Trip must be booked by December 31, 2001, and completed within one year of notification. No substitution of prize permitted by winner. Torstar Corp. and D. L. Blair, Inc., their parents, affiliates and subsidiaries are not responsible for errors in printing of contest, entries and/or game pieces. In the event of printing or other errors that may result in unintended prize values or duplication of prizes, all affected game pieces or entries shall be null and void. **Purchase or acceptance of a product offer does not improve your chances of winning.**

6. Prizes: (1) Grand Prize—A 2-night/3-day trip for two (2) to New York City, including round-trip coach air transportation nearest winner's home and hotel accommodations (double occupancy) at The Plaza Hotel, a glamorous afternoon makeover at a trendy New York spa, $1,000 in U.S. spending money and an opportunity to have a professional photo taken and appear in a Silhouette advertisement (approximate retail value: $7,000). (10) Ten Runner-Up Prizes of gift packages (retail value $50 ea.). Prizes consist of only those items listed as part of the prize. Limit one prize per person. Prize is valued in U.S. currency.

7. For the name of the winner (available after December 31, 2001) send a self-addressed, stamped envelope to: Harlequin "Silhouette Makes You a Star!" Contest 1197 Winners, P.O. Box 4200 Blair, NE 68009-4200 or you may access the www.eHarlequin.com Web site through February 28, 2002.

Contest sponsored by Torstar Corp., P.O Box 9042, Buffalo, NY 14269-9042.

COMING SOON...

AN EXCITING
OPPORTUNITY TO SAVE
ON THE PURCHASE OF
HARLEQUIN AND
SILHOUETTE BOOKS!

*DETAILS TO FOLLOW
IN OCTOBER 2001!*

YOU WON'T WANT TO MISS IT!

PHQ401

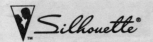

COMING NEXT MONTH

SSECNM0901